Murder in a Mask

PARTNERS IN SPYING MYSTERIES: BOOK THREE

ROSE DONOVAN

Moon Snail Press

For my readers

Murder in a Mask

Copyright © 2024 by ROSE DONOVAN

www.rosedonovan.com

Published by Moon Snail Press

Editing: Nicky Taylor Editing & Heddon Publishing

All rights reserved. No part of this book may be reproduced or transmitted in any form or by any means, electronic or mechanical, including photocopying, recording, or by any information storage and retrieval system without the written permission of the author and publisher.

All the characters in this book are fictitious, and any resemblance to actual persons living or dead is purely coincidental.

Cast of Characters at Chidden Park

Ruby Dove – Reading chemistry at Oxford. Designer and spy-sleuth on a mission to right colonial and fashion injustices.

Fina Aubrey-Havelock – Reading history at Oxford. Assistant seamstress to Ruby, and her best friend. Ready to defend Ruby at any cost.

Pixley Hayford – Shameless journalist on the hunt for a scoop. Always game for a Ruby and Fina adventure.

Pari Karan – Owner of Karan's Garage in Crickle Hythe, and mother of Etty Karan. A pugnacious figure wrapped in floaty drapery.

Etty Karan – Daughter of Pari Karan, with a frivolous though no-nonsense streak – like her mother.

Milo Judson – Owner of the Drowned Duck in Crickle Hythe, and father of Archie Judson. A former pilot with a penchant for risk-taking.

Archie Judson – Son of Milo Judson and friend to Etty Karan. Dressed as a little devil.

Miranda Oliver – The local chemist and siren. Rumoured to be a witch.

Callum Sinclair – Caretaker of Chidden Park and nephew of Geraldine Craven. Not one to suffer fools gladly.

Geraldine Craven – Owner of Chidden Park and aunt of Callum Sinclair. Perhaps not as forgetful as she seems.

Atina Kattos – Nurse to Geraldine Craven at Chidden Park. Dreams of becoming a student at Oxford one day.

Nigel Triggs – Baby-faced owner of the village stores and husband of Beryl Triggs. An incurable gossip.

Beryl Triggs – Organiser of the Chidden Park gala and wife of Nigel Triggs. A Good Works grenadier.

Alfreda Whittle – A chief inspector with the Oxfordshire police. Resembles your kindest aunt, except she's a detective.

Sheridan Ainsley – Chief Inspector Whittle's sergeant. A peculiar profession for such a posh young man.

The Skeleton – Your guess is as good as Fina's.

Tom Lattimore – The village postman who is sweet on Ruby.

Miss Datchworth – Standing in for Principal Laverton at Quenby College. An odious toad.

Principal Laverton – Principal of Quenby College. Ruby and Fina cannot wait until she returns from her holiday.

Bertie – Archie Judson's adorable yet permanently grumpy miniature schnauzer.

CHAPTER
One

"DO you know why you're here, Miss Aubrey-Havelock?"

Truth be told, it might be one of many reasons. Subversive activities? Involvement in murder cases? Both were plausible explanations.

But my ponderous thoughts were wasted. Miss Datchworth relished filling this airless college room with rhetorical questions.

"Are you familiar with the term 'rustication'?"

"I believe the Latin root is *rusticus*, meaning 'open land or country'."

"Don't be insolent, girl. I will not tolerate insubordination."

"Isn't the existence of Quenby women's college at Oxford the very definition of insubordination?"

Miss Datchworth's fist pummelled the desk, sending biscuit crumbs flying onto her starched jacket. "Enough! As you so aptly point out, *rusticus* means 'open country'. It is a state of retreat. Therefore, you will be retreating from Quenby College."

Her mouth looked like a newt crawling across her chalky face. Indeed, her demeanour was amphibious, from thick toad eyes to jerks of her head, to ostensibly catch a passing fly.

"Miss Aubrey-Havelock." She leaned forward, those bulbous

eyes peering quizzically at mine. "What flights of fancy are you entertaining?"

So she *was* sharper than she appeared.

"What have I done?" I leaned forward, digging my fingernails into her leather-edged desk. "Was it my involvement with those Cornish murders?"

She squared the papers underneath her gnarled hands. "Rustication is a temporary status, different from the colloquial 'sent down'. The process allows us time to conduct an inquiry into your activities. We will determine whether you are fit to continue at Quenby by the end of term."

I opened my mouth, but she held up a wagging finger. "Do not press me further on the matter. I am not at liberty to disclose anything more."

The ticking clock on the mantel had been soothing but now thrust its unwelcome rhythm into the heavy silence. But perhaps a moment of contemplation would soften Miss Datchworth, or at least loosen her lips.

In my best enquiring voice, I asked, "Has Miss Ruby Dove also been 'rusticated'?"

"I am not at liberty—"

A vast pit of bile in my stomach lurched up my oesophagus. "Tell me this. When is the principal returning?"

"The principal will return next term. Do not even consider contacting her – it will only lengthen your rustication." She rolled the *r* in "rustication", dwelling on the fineries of archaic administrative language.

There was a knock at the door.

Miss Datchworth rose from the desk, all five foot of her struggling to loom over me. "You will pack your bags and vacate your rooms at once."

"Perhaps I might—"

"You heard me, Miss Aubrey-Havelock. You will leave at once."

On the bus to Crickle Hythe, I wiped away tears and put on sunglasses. An old woman with a baked-apple face stared at me.

"No need for those things on a day like today, luv."

I hadn't the energy to argue with her on this grey-streaked autumn day. My grandmother said that what doesn't kill you makes you stronger. But she'd never tangled with an Oxford college administration.

I wasn't stronger. But my rage certainly gave me a reckless strength.

The bus lumbered to a halt, and I lugged my earthly possessions down the steps, bumping my case against my legs. My awkward bags and searing pain surely symbolised my complete and utter failure, and I found myself sinking into self-pity. The muddy canal pathway didn't help matters, as I had to brush leaves and dirt from my shoes every few metres.

After at least five near-falls onto the pathway, I finally arrived. Dejected flat clouds pushed through the naked branches scraping the roof of Ruby Dove's honeyed stone cottage. An assertive mewing met my ears, followed by an equally assertive nose-wiping on my tights.

I scooped up the fat, grey, golden-eyed cat. "Pasty! At least you're happy to see me."

I rubbed his ear and peered into the cottage. Between the red curtains, I spied absolutely nothing – no movement from within.

"Where is she, snookums?" I cooed, bouncing Pasty in my arms.

The cat tumbled to the ground and shot off towards a fisherman perched on the edge of the canal. His large floppy hat and an oversized brown waxed coat made him resemble a dejected scarecrow.

Leaving my bags on the stone-flagged path, I stepped carefully through the wet grass.

"Pardon," I said. "Have you seen the woman who lives in this cottage?"

He removed his hat and turned around.

I gasped.

"Ruby Dove! What on earth are you doing?"

"Feens. How good to see you," Ruby said flatly.

Her face sagged, her lips were cracked, and her eyelids stood firmly at half-mast. And she wore no make-up – Ruby Dove without lipstick was like a cat without a purr. Absolutely inconceivable.

"Why are you fishing?" I asked. "And in this get-up?"

She pushed back her kerchief. "It passes the time, and I've had a few nibbles."

"Were you rusticated, too?"

She nodded. "Just as well. Doubt we'd ever finish, anyway. Not at the rate we were going."

A fish bobbed in the water, sending ripples a few inches from Ruby's line.

I pointed. "Did you see that?"

"What?"

"A fish, you goose. Right next to your rod."

"Oh."

Time to rally the troops. Or rather, the students.

"Where's your fighting spirit?" I gave her a playful nudge. "Weren't John Milton, Oscar Wilde, and Percy Shelley all rusticated? I fancy we've joined a distinguished cohort, haven't we?"

"Mmph."

"Don't you want to know why we've been sent down?"

Ruby's floppy hat sagged further, completely covering her eyes.

I frowned. I'd never seen her in such a state. Dreadful clothes, no make-up. And fishing? Never.

Behind me, footsteps crunched the pea-shingled pathway.

"Morning, miss," rumbled the boyish postman. Whilst his

walrus moustache gleamed with health, it still looked like it had been affixed with spirit gum.

"Morning, Tom," mumbled Ruby. "You've met Fina, haven't you?"

His freckled white face blushed as red as his postbag. "Oh, y-yes."

I smiled. Tom had a bit of a pash on Ruby.

"Caught anything?" he asked, duly ignoring my presence.

"Just a few nibbles," she replied.

"I've got a minute," he said. "And I have a fishing secret to share. But I'll need to take your rod."

Ruby handed it to him, her shoulders slumping further. "Go on," she murmured.

This was ludicrous. I simply had to act, so I dashed towards the cottage, only hindered twice by Pasty tripping me up. Inside, I found the telephone and rang the operator, praying my friend would be at home.

Breathless, I wheezed, "Pixley! Thank goodness I caught you."

"Well hello to you, too. What's the matter, Red? Why are you panting? Do you have a story for me?"

"I have a story, but not one for the paper."

"Red, dearest, I'm on a deadline, so please don't dawdle. You do waffle on sometimes."

"I do not!"

"That's true, actually. Sometimes you just blurt things out."

"Well, I'll practise my blurting skills now: Ruby is in trouble."

Pixley chuckled. "Not that kind of trouble, surely."

"Pixley Hayford, you can be positively exasperating. She's, well, not herself."

"In what way?"

"For one thing, she's fishing."

"Great Scott! She threatened to do it, but she's actually outside, with a rod?"

"As we speak. And that postman is showing her how to do it."

"I'm sure he is. That postie definitely has designs on her."

"She's not wearing make-up, and to top it off, she's wearing this misshapen brown blobby wax get-up."

"Wax? What, is she preparing to be put into Madame Tussaud's?"

"Never mind. I've never seen her like this. It's because we've been rusticated, of course, but normally she'd be ready to fight."

"Ah, the old rustication wheeze. Practised by Oscar Wilde, I believe."

"This is no time for jokes, Pix. We must do something, and quickly, before she takes up knitting those endless scarves, like sweet village ladies do."

"Most dire, I agree. Perhaps a distraction is in order?"

"Such as?"

Lip-smacking echoed from the receiver. "Well, besides her chemistry degree, Ruby's first love is designing clothes. Maybe we could use that to distract her somehow? Perhaps some duchess is hankering for a splendid new ballgown."

For the first time, I surveyed my surroundings. A leaning tower of dishes threatened to smash into the kitchen sink. A sour, foul odour hung about the room. Newspapers were strewn about, and even Ruby's favourite mannequin had jumpers and jackets piled on top. It was dire indeed.

Then my eye settled on an orange scrap of paper underneath a teacup. It read "Halloween Gala, Chidden Park, 31 October".

"Are you there, Red?" called Pixley's voice.

"Sorry. I was reading about a Halloween gala at Chidden Park."

"Isn't Chidden Park the manor house on the outskirts of Crickle Hythe?" Through the receiver, I heard him snap his fingers. "Bingo! It's a village fancy dress party, so why don't you ask Ruby to design the fancy dress for the guests?"

"Brilliant idea, Pix!"

I looked up. Footsteps approached, and the door creaked open.

"I must go," I hissed.

Ruby shuffled through the door.

"Who were you speaking to?" she asked without interest.

"Pixley. Just seeing if he wants to visit us soon."

She slumped onto the sofa, not even bothering to move the pile of blankets in her way.

"Maybe I'll take a nap," she said.

I held up the scrap of paper. "Are you going to this Halloween gala at Chidden Park? It looks amusing, and you could meet more of your neighbours."

She waved her arm and let it plop onto her lap. "Why bother?"

I took a deep breath, searching for patience and an idea. Outside on the window ledge, Pasty flicked his tail and flattened his ears, probably readying to pounce on a poor sleepy dormouse.

An idea finally came to me. "I've got it!"

"What have you got, Feens?"

"Did you hear about the hedgehogs?"

Ruby stiffened.

Now, Ruby Dove was a perfect human in every way, except when the subject of hedgehogs arose. She was absolutely petrified of the little roly-polies.

"Glad I have your attention," I said. "Are you aware of the new building plans at Chidden Park?"

Her eyelids fell again to half-mast. "I haven't a clue."

"They're going to make it into a hedgehog farm! They're going to breed them by the dozen! By the thousands!"

"Selkies and kelpies!" Ruby jumped onto the sofa in her stockinged feet, as if the little beasties had already toddled down from Chidden Park and were streaming through the front door, ready to taunt her.

But the reality was quite different: it was Pasty dashing through the front door.

Ruby grabbed him and cuddled him in her arms. "You wouldn't let the nasty vermin come here, would you, sweetie?"

He wriggled from her arms and shot into the garden, ready to defend against the hordes.

Ruby brushed her hands together and slipped on her shoes.

"Right," she said. "I'll change upstairs whilst you make us tea. Then we'll go to Chidden Park to give them a piece of my mind. Hedgehogs indeed."

CHAPTER
Two

RUBY JABBED THE BELL. One long ring, then two short ones.

"I think that's plenty," I said, glancing over the hedge protecting Chidden Park's garden. Weeds proudly lined the stone-flagged path, defying any gardener to remove them. And the hedges sprouted everywhere, like exuberant mushrooms.

With pursed lips, Ruby pressed the bell one more time.

I sighed. "Perhaps they're not at home."

She stamped her foot. "I'll write to the council. No, I'll write to the Chancellor of Oxford. He'll want to be informed of this plan to blight our peaceful country landscape."

"I'm certain he'll share your outrage."

We strolled along the drive, kicking pebbles in frustration.

"Pardon me, did you ring the bell?" came a voice behind us.

Ruby spun round and dashed up the steps. "We thought you weren't at home."

"Well, there aren't many of us rattling about this pile." The woman at the door gestured to the garden. "As you'll notice, plenty of things must be seen to."

Ruby stuck out her hand. "I'm Ruby Dove, and this is Fina Aubrey-Havelock. Is this your house?"

Her question was a matter of politeness, as the woman at the door wore a crisp white nurse's uniform. Though her thick raven hair was in a plait so tight it pulled her arched eyebrows upwards, she still managed to register surprise.

"No, I'm Nurse Kattos. Do come in."

She ushered us into a musty hall with cracked oil paintings of dead pheasants, and mirrors so old they were speckled with brown spots.

"Wait here. I'll find Callum."

I removed my hat and unbuttoned my coat.

"Don't bother, Feens," said Ruby. "I'll say my piece and then we'll leave."

I couldn't help myself. "What piece might that be, then?"

A small, bony man swaggered into the room with his arms crossed and tongue pushing into his left cheek.

"Pleased to meet you," said Ruby. "I'm Ruby Dove and this is my friend, Fina Aubrey-Havelock. I'm your neighbour."

His arms remained crossed. "The name's Callum. Callum Sinclair," he said in a rasping, light Scottish accent.

I squeezed my hat between my hands, suddenly consumed with worry. How could I be such an idiot? I'd been so pleased with my scheme to revive the wilting Ruby Dove that I hadn't considered what would actually happen when we discussed the imaginary hedgehog farm.

"Mr Sinclair." Ruby held her chin high. "I'm a newcomer to Crickle Hythe, but as a new resident, I'm confident you'll understand my concerns about your plans."

"Plans?"

"The hedgehog farm."

His arms dropped. "The hedgehog farm," he said flatly.

"Yes. The one you're planning for Chidden Park."

Callum scratched the stubble on his chin. "I'm a newcomer here, like yourself, Miss Dove. And I'm looking after Lady Geraldine, my aunt. So this is the first I've heard of plans for a ... hedgehog farm. As adorable as the beasties might be."

"So there's no farm? No hedgehogs?"

"Only the ones wandering our bedraggled estate. If you walk around the grounds, you'll spot a few."

Ruby shuddered. "No, no. That's fine."

The lines on Callum's forehead remained arched, though they now conveyed genuine interest rather than disbelief. And possibly amusement.

"Tell me," he said, "who gave you this information?"

Ruby turned to me. "Where did you hear it from, Fina?"

I had dug myself into a trench fit for Ruby's vegetable patch. She had said "Fina" instead of "Feens", which meant she'd already rumbled my little charade.

Thankfully, a smashing sound echoed across the wooden floors, saving me from offering a fumbling answer.

"That'll be Aunt Geraldine, no doubt." Callum dashed from the room, and we had no choice but to follow.

We wound through the corridor lined with threadbare rugs and dust-covered bric-a-brac. The house had a definite earthen decaying smell – not unpleasant, but persistent in its declaration of age.

Callum turned into the conservatory: a light-filled, lush jungle rather than a conventional room with pot plants. I could see why anyone would want to escape the English autumn chill in such a warm and tropical environment.

White shards of a former china vase were strewn around an elderly woman in a wheelchair, presumably Lady Geraldine. Tousled white hair framed a long, judgemental face, intensified by sharp eyes peeking out beneath her fringe. Her knitted spiderweb lace shawl was held together at her neck with a large diamond brooch.

"You stupid girl," she croaked. "See what you've done. Again."

Nurse Kattos's plait swung in vigorous denial. "You have an injection every day, Lady Geraldine. Why put up such a fuss?"

The subject of their dispute sat in a case on an occasional table: a gleaming, half-full syringe.

Lady Geraldine continued her monologue. "And that equally stupid doctor can go hang himself. He had the nerve to ask me to vote for him in the council election. Nothing but a quack if you ask me."

Nurse Kattos brushed her hands against her apron. "If you prefer to forget your injection, Aunt Geraldine, it doesn't matter to me."

"Don't call me Aunt! It's Lady Geraldine to you."

She crooked a withered finger at Callum, her impassive face softening. "Dear Callum, I believe it's time to find another nurse."

"Auntie, you know that's impossible. Nurse Kattos is a godsend."

She gave a lively snort. "God-sent from Cyprus. Preposterous."

Nurse Kattos was already rolling up Lady Geraldine's sleeve. "Preposterous? If your preposterous country hadn't invaded mine, I wouldn't be here."

"Are you calling the British Empire preposterous?"

Nurse Kattos jabbed the needle into Lady Geraldine's arm. "There." She glanced at Callum. "I fancy the Scots feel the same way as the Cypriots."

Callum clapped as if he'd just seen a thrilling West End show. "Well done, well done, you two. A perfect performance for our guests. If you will excuse the interruption, I'd like you to meet two of our neighbours, a Miss Dove and Miss Aubrey—"

"Aubrey-Havelock," I put in.

"Are they here to help with the gala?" asked Lady Geraldine. "Because that pushy woman from the village stores has already become a martyr for the cause."

"No, we're—" Ruby said.

"Actually, what she means is yes," I interjected. "We're here to help out with the fancy dress, aren't we, Ruby?"

CHAPTER
Three

THE NIGHT of the Halloween gala was upon us, and our plan had worked beautifully. Ruby Dove was back on form, resplendent in her red, figure-hugging Isis costume.

I closed my eyes and rubbed green eyeshadow on my lids. "Remind me of who Isis is. I was absent the day they discussed gods and goddesses at school."

"Isis was wise—"

"Naturally."

"And she was a magician who crafted clever plots to fool her enemies."

With dismay, I surveyed my green tights and leather skirt. "Whereas my outfit …"

"Nonsense. The Robin Hood outfit suits you, Feens." Ruby dipped her wand into her mascara. "Much better than the dormouse from *Alice in Wonderland*."

"That dormouse helmet was too hot and sticky."

"And you couldn't hear a thing."

"But isn't this Robin Hood get-up a bit revealing?"

She waved a hand at me in the looking glass. "You're absolutely smashing, Feens."

I rose from Ruby's dressing table and peeked through the curtains. "No sign of Pixley yet. He said he had a surprise for us."

"Of course. It's Pix, so there must be a surprise."

"It's already half five, and Mrs Triggs told you to be early to help out," I said.

Her busy mascara wand stopped. "Mrs Triggs can go to the devil."

"She really has irked you, hasn't she?"

"Mrs Triggs is the most interfering busybody I've ever met. And believe me, I've met more than my share of do-gooders."

"Well, you're a do-gooder yourself, aren't you?"

"I suppose, but when she insisted I couldn't come as Isis because it was too pagan, that was the last straw."

"But Halloween *is* pagan."

"My point precisely."

Three gunshots echoed through the open window. I drew back the curtains and peered outside. "I expect someone is taking potshots at rabbits."

"I suspect it was Callum and his apple-howling plans."

"Pardon?"

Ruby rose and put on her long camel-hair coat. "I forgot you weren't present for the little committee meeting. Callum is using his gun collection for the apple howling."

"Which is? Is it like apple wassailing?"

"Yes. It normally happens in the New Year, but Callum wanted it to coincide with this gala, since his apple orchard – or rather, Lady Geraldine's orchard – has literally gone to seed."

"What does this have to do with rifles?"

"The tradition is to pour apple cider on the roots of the trees and on bits of bread tied to the tree. Then you fire guns through the tree branches."

"Only batty country people could concoct such a scheme," I said, momentarily forgetting I was raised in such a batty landscape myself.

"It is delightfully batty," Ruby tinkled. "Anyway, here's the story: you scare away evil spirits with the gunshots. And the cider heals the trees, so you'll have a bumper crop come next autumn."

"Are you telling me we're going to stand outside in the mud and watch people fire rifles into the freezing air?"

"Where's your spirit of adventure?"

I suddenly became grumpy for no apparent reason. "It disappeared with the sunny weather a few months ago. This weather is for staying at home."

A splashing noise came from outside.

"See?" I said with perverse triumph in my voice. "Rotten luck – the rain is coming down in sheets. We'll have to cancel this howling."

Ruby surveyed the window. "Darling Feens, that's not rain."

"Pixley Hayford!" I cried.

"But, soft! What light through yonder window breaks? It is the east, and Juliet is the sun. Arise, fair sun, and kill the envious moon."

Ruby leaned out of the window and clasped her chest. "Ay me! Romeo!"

"All right, you two." I crossed my arms, peering down at Pixley. He had a kerchief tied around his head and wore a leather jerkin with a puffy white shirt.

"Tell us what you're playing at, Mr Hayford," I said.

He flung his arm at the narrowboat moored near Ruby's cottage. "I've come to whisk you away, dear Red. What do you think?"

"It's yours?" I squealed. "I've always wanted a narrowboat!"

"Well, you're welcome anytime. Come down, dear friends. Your carriage awaits."

I flung on my coat, and we hurried from the cottage. I hopped across the plank set into the bank and stepped tentatively on board the delightful green-and-red boat, complete with a skull-and-crossbones flag flapping at the front. The bow sported curly gold lettering reading *Queen Anne's Revenge*.

"What on earth made you buy this?" I said, pushing open the double doors and marvelling at the gleaming wooden interior.

"Blasted London rents, that's what. So I traded in my flat in the Big Smoke for this sweetheart. My idea is to amble around to find delectable scoops for the *Daily Rumble*."

I stepped down into the dining area, but not before I slipped on the purple velvet cushions that lay across a U-shaped bench.

"Watch your step, Red. Narrowboats require a bit more attention and fancy footwork."

"There's nothing wrong with my footwork," I huffed. Then I squealed with delight as my eyes alighted on the tiny stove and perfectly arranged teacups on the layered shelves above it.

"Spiffing folding bed, Pix," said Ruby, turning back from the bedroom at the far end of the boat. "And now you can visit us."

"Precisely, dear Isis," he said. "You look rather fetching as an Egyptian goddess."

Then he eyed me. "Erm, what are you going as, Red? *Haricot vert?*"

Ruby snorted, suppressing a laugh. "If she looks like a vegetable, it's entirely my fault. Our original dormouse idea was a disaster, so I suggested Robin Hood."

"Ah, ye merry men of Sherwood Forest." He gave an exaggerated bow. "Well, you're in good company, since I'm going as Black Caesar, the pirate. Actually, his name was Henri and he was part of the Haitian revolution."

"Delightful," I said flatly. "Let's go."

Pixley's nose twitched. "I do believe our dear green vegetable is peckish. What say you, Ruby?"

"I'm always prepared." She whipped out a packet of chocolate digestives.

I tore into the packet and gulped the first one. It was completely ridiculous that Ruby carried biscuits for me like I was a toddler, but needs must.

"Much better," I said. "Full speed ahead, Captain Ahab."

Pixley expertly piloted the narrowboat through the darkness, lit only by occasional houses along the canal. A light breeze prompted me to go inside, but a firm hand held me back.

"Almost there, Red," said Pixley.

"Why do I have two nicknames, and Ruby has none?" I ask. I'm genuinely curious.

"I see you're still peckish," said Pixley.

"It's a legitimate question, Pix," said Ruby. "But the shortened form of my name would be 'Rube', which isn't the most flattering, is it?"

"True enough," said Pixley. "And it's not like your name is Ethelred, which could be Etty, Ethel, or Red."

"An old school chum once tried to call me "Pi," said Pixley, "but I soon put a stop to that."

"Talking of pie," I said, "do you think there will be things like that at the gala?"

"I've heard village gossip that Crickle Hythe is a place that loves to eat."

"Well then, I thoroughly approve of your decision to live here," I laugh.

A moment later, our trusty boat scraped the edge of the canal outside Chidden Park.

My feet crunched brown leaves up the footpath leading to the back gate. Through the dense foliage, I spotted the warm glow of the house beyond, and the apple orchard next to it. Voices floated from the house – Mrs Triggs's being the most obvious amongst them.

"No, no, no, Milo. Put it there!"

Ruby's lips pursed into a grim line. "Mrs Triggs is in fine form."

"What's this?" asked Pixley as he tied up the boat.

"Village characters," said Ruby.

"Ah well," said Pixley. "It will make a welcome change from the London crowd."

Ruby sighed. "Don't be too sure, El Capitan, don't be too sure."

CHAPTER
Four

"THERE YOU ARE, Miss Dove! I thought you'd never arrive. Did you know it's already twenty-two minutes past six?"

Mrs Nigel Triggs – or "Beryl" to those who dared – bore down on us. Her prim and frozen smile was so common among efficient women: a mixture of patience and niceness masking complete exasperation. Mrs Triggs undoubtedly found every moment of her waking life to be a sore trial.

Ruby gritted her teeth. "A pleasure to see you as well, Mrs Triggs. Now, how can we be of assistance?"

Mrs Triggs spun round and clapped her hands. "Nurse Kattos, would you take those apples to the children?"

Ruby rolled her eyes at Mrs Triggs's back.

The kitchen at Chidden Park buzzed with activity. Large vats of savoury and sweet-smelling concoctions bubbled on the vast range. A village woman popped open the oven, revealing two moist seed cakes for the festivities. A mound of shiny apples sat next to carved, toothless swedes, ready to brave the chill outside to ward off evil spirits.

A small devil scampered across the chequerboard marble floor and out the back door.

"Who was that?" asked Pixley.

"Archie Judson, Milo Judson's son," said Ruby.

"Did you call my name?"

A man in a Roman warrior costume strode towards us.

"We did indeed, sir," said Pixley in a mischievous whisper.

"I'm Milo Judson, owner of the Drowned Duck."

He gripped my hand so tightly I winced.

Milo grinned. "And the little devil running about is my son."

Pixley pumped Milo's hand, not letting it go. "How do you do?"

Milo was frightfully handsome, and he used his bare-chested costume to emphasise his excellent physique. He wore his thick hair like a helmet, covering his ears and edging towards his greying temples. But his rather sinister Mephistophelean peaked eyebrows made him more than a pretty face. And I never trusted anyone with teeth that white.

Mrs Triggs re-entered the room and clapped her hands. "Has anyone seen Pari? She promised to put the apples on string for the children."

A roly-poly woman in a butterfly costume floated into the room. "I'm here, Beryl. I was just fixing the children's fancy dress."

"Pari, you haven't put out the carved swedes with the candles yet," said Beryl. Or rather, Mrs Triggs.

"Beryl," said Pari in a low voice. "I'm not your servant. And if you take that tone with me again, I'll boil your head in the soup on the stove. Do you understand me?"

Mrs Triggs tittered nervously and pushed back her grey-brown curls. "You are most amusing, Pari. Most amusing." Then she turned her back on Pari and marched into the corridor.

Pari gave out an emphatic "Bloody hell," and floated away in her swirl of draperies.

"Who was that?" I asked Ruby.

"Pari runs the local garage. She's quite alarming, but harmless really."

Milo stretched out his arms. "Pari is right. If that damn Triggs tells me how to pull a pint of beer one more time, I may well blast her with one of Callum's rifles."

Archie dashed in and skidded to a halt, tugging his father's cape. "Dad! Come and see the flaming torches they're lighting outside!"

"Not now, son. I'm busy."

Archie looked up at his father, his drawn-on moustache looking significantly better than Pixley's pirate effort. Finally relenting, Milo let the little devil lead him outside.

"Archie's false moustache is better than yours, Pix," I said.

"What do you mean, 'false moustache'?"

"Is it real?" I gasped.

Ruby grabbed Pixley and stared at his face. "It's real, all right."

Pixley smoothed the bristles, which ended well before the edges of his mouth.

I couldn't help myself. "It looks remarkably like a certain dictator who shall remain nameless."

Pixley squinted over the top of his spectacles. "And you're still behaving this way after Ruby fed you, Red?"

"Feens is right, Pix," said Ruby. "The moustache is rather catastrophic."

He caressed it once more. "I'd like to oblige you ladies, but I'm afraid the old soup strainer shall stay firmly affixed to my upper lip."

A tiny witch flew in from the corridor on her broom, riding it like a horse. She zipped between Pixley and me, sending a jug of tomato juice hurtling to the floor. It missed Pixley, but the fine red mist splattered my green tights and skirt.

"Selkies and kelpies!" I yelled.

Everyone in the kitchen turned around. I couldn't tell if they were more startled by the accident or my choice of words.

Ruby rushed to my side. "Do you need help?"

"No, no," I grumbled, surveying the damage. "I'll find the toilet and will fix this."

She eyed my tights sceptically. "I don't think you can fix it. You'd better put on another costume."

I groaned. "What's left? That blasted dormouse? Or how about the pig costume I spotted earlier? Then my general humiliation can be complete."

"Rubbish. Besides, the village butcher is already dressed in the pig get-up. No, all that's left is a Marie Antoinette outfit upstairs. You'll be smashing in it, but ..."

"But what?"

"Well, you'll see if you like it," she mumbled.

"I haven't much choice, have I? It's that or going naked."

Pixley winked. "I would approve of such a daring option, of course, but I fancy these country people might burn you at the stake."

Ruby ignored him. "If you want the costume, it's upstairs in the trunk in the smallest bedroom."

She held up her wristwatch. "You'd better rush, since it's almost time to meet outside for the apple howling. And those dreadful rifles."

CHAPTER
Five

CHIDDEN PARK HAD TRANSFORMED itself from its melancholy, shabby shell into a warm and lively house. Jazz blared from the conservatory, where young people threw themselves about with abandon to the drumbeat of Duke Ellington. Shrieks of joy echoed in the corridors.

As I passed the library, I spotted a witch supervising the apple-bobbing with the younger children. She'd hung a long string from the ceiling and attached an apple. A girl dressed as a bumblebee buzzed round the apple, snapping at it with her little teeth.

A quieting sense of escape erased the frenetic energy downstairs as I climbed the groaning staircase. A jester jingled past me, tripping lightly down the steps. A pink-and-purple fairy followed him, her two pigtails swinging with child-like abandon.

I reached the landing and scanned the corridor, wondering which door led to what Ruby had called the "smallest bedroom".

One door had a knob that stuck. Another revealed an upstairs bathroom. Each room was dustier than the last, and the decor was stuck in time, probably from at least thirty or forty years ago. In an old nursery, flowered wallpaper peeled like orange zest from the wall.

The fifth room smelled of rosewater. I remembered from our

previous visit that Lady Geraldine wore rosewater, just like my grandmother did.

Shaking myself from a pleasant walk down memory lane, I scanned the room, searching for a trunk. None was to be found, but a large velvet-covered box caught my eye.

It wouldn't hurt to have a peek, would it?

With one glance over my shoulder to ensure no one was about, I lifted the lid.

Inside sat an exquisite array of brooches inlaid with precious stones, much like the one Lady Geraldine was wearing on our ill-fated 'hedgehog farm' excursion. The coloured stones sparkled and flashed: ruby, sapphire, and emerald.

A floorboard creaked and a voice arose behind me.

"Did you find what you were after, Miss Aubrey-Havelock?"

I dropped the lid of the jewellery case, banging it on my hand. Writhing in pain, I did my best to turn my wince into a smile.

The intruder was Callum. He strode towards me in a tattered brown peasant-like outfit, holding a long green stalk with a candle tied to the top.

Even in my flustered state, I noticed how peculiar it was.

"Oh, I, ah," I said, somewhere between embarrassment and puzzlement. "I was just looking for a cigarette."

"I don't smoke," he said.

"Oh well then, I'll be off." I turned to go.

He opened the box and turned his grey eyes on me. "Where's my aunt's diamond brooch?"

"Perhaps she's wearing it?" I offered, not even believing my own words as I said them.

He pointed to another empty spot in the box. "No, she's wearing the yellow sapphire tonight."

It was time for a distraction. "Why are you carrying that vegetable? Is it kale? And why is a candle tied to it?"

He lifted it and peered at it as if seeing it for the first time.

"This? Oh, aye. It's kale, and I'm dressed as the Cromartie Fool."

I stared blankly at him.

"You know, the jester of the laird. The one who looks over Halloween gatherings like ours. The poet Robbie Burns wrote about it. Surely you're familiar with Robbie Burns?"

Without waiting for my reply, he said, "Don't distract me. Where's the brooch?"

"Honestly, I was simply searching for another fancy-dress costume to replace my soiled one. Ruby said the trunk was in the smallest bedroom upstairs, so I had to try each room because I didn't know which was the smallest."

"And so temptation overcame you in Aunt Geraldine's bedroom."

I let out a squawk of frustration, sending him reeling a few steps backwards.

Worried that I now appeared more unhinged than ever, I pointed to my green-and-red tights. "Look at me. Can't you see I had an accident with tomato juice?"

His steady gaze told me this still wasn't enough, so I tried again. "See this outfit? How could I hide a diamond brooch the size of Mount Snowdon on my person?"

His eyes flickered up and down, crinkling up with amusement. "Aye. You have a point. But you might have simply stuffed it into your unmentionables."

My face flamed, undoubtedly the colour of that blasted tomato juice. I had to do something. "Here's a proposal. You give me the Marie Antoinette costume Ruby told me about, and I'll change behind a screen – if you have one. You're welcome to stand on the other side of the screen and to wait. Then we can clear up this dratted business."

He crossed his arms. "Fine. We'll do just that, shall we?"

"Oh, I—"

He gave a quick snort. "You didn't think I'd take you up on your little offer, did you?"

Callum was quite right.

He held out a hand as if we were agreeing to a wager.

"Challenge accepted, Mr Sinclair." Deciding he wasn't going to get the better of me, I crossed my arms and marched out of the room.

Soon I was flipping my damp, smelly clothes over the top of a screen in a draughty room across from Lady Geraldine's. When it came to my unmentionables, I tentatively slipped them over the side as evidence for Callum and then hurriedly slipped them back. It was the best I could do without submitting to a full-body search, which was certainly out of the question.

"Are you satisfied?" I called.

"Aye," said Callum. "Almost. I'll wait until you're finished."

Crumbs. The man was deuced insistent.

With tremendous effort, I hauled on the Marie Antoinette costume. How on earth did women do this every day? Corsets were clearly the devil. I'd need to ask Ruby to tie up the back, although the laces were already making it difficult to breathe.

Finally, I threw on a scratchy white-blonde wig and stepped from behind the screen.

Callum smirked. "Well, you won't be hiding any brooches in there, will you?"

Then he took my hand and shook it. "Apologies, and thank you for bearing with my unusual request. I'll have to alert the police about the missing brooch."

"Can't you ask Lady Geraldine? Maybe she put it somewhere?"

He scratched his head. "I would, except she's senile. That's why I'm here, since it's become worse. And Nurse Kattos, too. Bless her, she's the only one who'll put up with Auntie."

He gave a little bow like he was avoiding hitting his head on a low beam, and made a quick exit.

Leaving me in front of the looking glass.

I stared at myself in horror.

To say I had cleavage would be the understatement of the year. Good Lord. I couldn't go downstairs like this, so I began shifting around in the corset, thrashing about like one of Ruby's poor fish on the line.

And then, in a final act of mockery from the gods, the lights went out.

CHAPTER
Six

AT FIRST, the darkness prompted whoops of delight and thrilled shrieks from downstairs. But after a minute or two, the tone changed. Shuffling footsteps and rising mumbling echoed up the stairs.

With my fingertips brushing the wall, I'd crept from the windowless room into the corridor, where light filtered in from the windows at each end.

I groped along the wall, trying to remember if I'd noticed a torch or candlelight anywhere. My fingers touched the glass doorknob to Lady Geraldine's room, something I'd admired before. The door was ajar, although I was certain Callum had locked it after discovering the missing brooch.

With one forefinger, I nudged the door open further. Surely there'd be a torch or a candle. Then a cold breeze ruffled my wig. The window with the moonlight filtering in was open – perhaps that's why the door was ajar.

As my eyes adjusted to the darkness, I spotted a candlestick on a tallboy in the corner. Halfway across the floor, my arm brushed against something smooth in the middle of the room.

I took another step and yelped. The smooth object had grabbed my wrist.

"Shh," came a voice.

A clicking noise was followed by a yellow flame. The figure held the lighter up to my face. I squirmed backwards, wrestling my wrist from the tight grip.

"Stop. That's right, I won't hurt you," whispered the figure, removing any individuality from the voice. "My, Marie Antoinette suits you."

Though the figure was backlit, it was still difficult to see. The chest had white lines on it, glowing in the dark. Then I focused on the head. It was a skull.

Terrified, I stamped my foot, here, there, and everywhere. Thank goodness I'd exchanged my Robin Hood slippers for my Marie Antoinette heels with pointy toes. With all my strength, I kicked my shoe at the figure.

A yell and a groan came from the skeleton. The lighter went out but I spied the figure limping towards the window.

Emboldened, I yelled, "Come back here!"

The skeleton crawled along the windowsill, stepping onto a ladder propped against the house. It turned and faced me once more, the white lines of the skull glowing in the silver light before disappearing below.

A shaft of moonlight lit up my shoes and a scrap of paper.

I picked it up and patted my gown, searching for a pocket. But of course Marie Antoinette wouldn't need pockets – she'd order some poor underling to carry everything for her.

So I shoved the paper into my bosom. Fortunately, I still had enough sense to chuckle at the absurdity of this situation.

And then the lights flickered, pulsed, and finally returned me to a semblance of normality. Except for my ridiculous get-up.

"Here, Feens." Ruby handed me a red shawl. "You'll catch a cold outside if you don't cover up."

"That's not all she'll catch," Pixley tittered. "Being naked might have been less provocative."

"Ha jolly ha ha." I pulled the shawl over my neck and chest.

"Sorry," said Ruby. "You can see why I didn't suggest this costume for you in the first place."

"We can't leave Red alone for a minute, can we?" Pixley continued chuckling. "First, she's accused of jewel theft, then she transforms into a vamp, and then tangles with a skeleton in the dark."

"Yes, well," I said. "It does sound daft now that you say it. I wouldn't believe it myself."

"Ignore Pixley," said Ruby. "He's miffed because Milo isn't dancing around him with adoring eyes."

"Ah, well, I'm certain Milo will soon, Pix. After all, he's occupied with his little devil."

Pixley blew out his cheeks. "I'm positive I spotted that gleam in his eye."

Ruby slipped on a glittering gold shawl and pulled it round her neck. "They're waiting for us outside. Let's go."

We meandered through the busy kitchen, sidestepping chatting couples, marauding little goblins, and an adorable stuffed bear. In the doorway, I collided with a jester.

"Sorry. I haven't got the hang of these skirts yet," I apologised.

I squinted at his half-covered face. Surely I'd seen him earlier. "Weren't you on the stairs before the lights went out?"

A bell from his fool's hat dangled near my nose. "I'm afraid I didn't notice. The only person I saw was Robin Hood covered in tomato juice."

"That was me, before I changed. I'm Fina Aubrey-Havelock."

"Pleased to meet you. I'm Nigel Triggs."

He pulled off his jester's cap. What remained of his light, downy hair framed his baby face in a beige halo, matching his beige skin. His rimless mouth also puckered, smiled, and opened much like a baby after a satisfying meal.

"Of course, I ought to have recognised you," I said. "You run the village stores with Mrs Triggs."

"Yes, yes," he agreed. "My dear wife has done a simply splendid job at organising this bash, hasn't she?"

"Oh yes, absolutely spiffing."

Dear Lord, nature did work in mysterious ways. How could he have such affection for a woman as insufferable as Mrs Triggs?

He sipped his punch. "Did you hear that Lady Geraldine's brooch has been stolen?"

I let my Marie Antoinette skirts drop as fast as my stomach.

"Who told you that?" I asked in an overly casual manner.

"I was minding my own business, but I happened to overhear Callum – Mr Sinclair – asking his aunt where she'd put her brooch. She said someone had stolen it."

"Did she suspect someone of pinching it?"

Nigel was walking near me, bobbing and weaving as if he were afraid of being overheard.

"Lady Geraldine said it had to be Nurse Kattos, but she would say that, wouldn't she?"

"Look here, Nigel," I said. "Would you mind keeping this story under your hat? At least for now?"

"Well, I …"

Summoning my most winsome smile, I said, "I knew you'd understand. Just until the gala is over. Trust me, I have my reasons."

"Reasons?" asked the witch I'd spotted earlier in the library. She sauntered towards us in a silver-streaked tight-fitting gown, no mean feat given the state of the slippery pathway.

"Hullo, Miranda," said Nigel. "I was saying that Lady Geraldine—"

"Is so fortunate to have Callum and Nurse Kattos looking after her," I put in.

"If only Lady Geraldine appreciated them more. Or at least Nurse Kattos." Miranda leaned forward, popping her head past Nigel. "I'm Miranda Oliver. The local witch."

"And she means it!" giggled Nigel. Perhaps he had been hitting the punch a bit too hard.

We finally reached the apple orchard, where Nigel toddled off towards his wife.

Miranda held out her cigarette case. "Gasper?"

"I'll have one." Pixley bounded up. "Thanks. Fabulous costume. It's Miss Oliver, right? Ruby mentioned you're the chemist."

"Well done. And you must be Pixley Hayford. I've read your stories, especially the ones on Ethiopia."

"Good show." Pixley launched into a monologue on Ethiopia, giving me a chance to survey Miranda more closely. Her sharp eyebrows flinched at all the right moments in Pixley's story. Every look and twitch was as carefully planned as her beautifully made-up face.

Clearly, it wouldn't do to underestimate Miranda Oliver.

I stood back as Mrs Triggs's tenor voice cracked through Pixley's stream of words. "Everyone, everyone, may I have your attention."

Ruby joined our growing circle.

I leaned over and whispered, "Why isn't Mrs Triggs wearing fancy dress?"

Ruby flicked lint from her sleeve. "She said she's only a humble servant."

"Priceless, isn't she?"

I stared through the bare tree branches at the full moon on this blue-grey night. The orchard stretched out before us, full of naked and depressed apple trees. A dove swooped and sailed past us, alighting on a wooden dovecote at the far end of the orchard. It was indeed the perfect Halloween.

We stood in a muddy, fenced-in enclosure, set off from the back of the glowing house. With the help of Milo and Pari, Mr Triggs was unloading a cart of cider jugs – the Roman, the butterfly, and the jester working together as if this were a Lewis Carroll story.

Callum had left behind his kale and was polishing his rifles.

Mrs Triggs directed the cider jug operation, whilst Miranda and Pixley chatted with Lady Geraldine. Nurse Kattos stood to the side, puffing on a cigarette as if it were a sour medicinal remedy.

"What's next?" I asked Ruby.

She shivered and pointed at Callum. "I don't like guns, Feens."

"Nor do I. But it is all rather exciting."

I gulped my drink, letting it mellow my jangled nerves.

But the effect vanished when Ruby grabbed my arm and pointed at the house.

CHAPTER
Seven

A LINE of burning torches waved in the dark, a disembodied, ghostlike queue of red and yellow. Perhaps it was meant to be awe-inspiring, but I simply found it menacing.

Pixley's cigarette fell from his lips onto the wet grass. "Good Lord! What are they doing?"

Callum jumped onto the wooden cart. "Welcome, everyone, to our new Halloween tradition. Apple howling, or apple wassailing, as it's called, is a tradition in many parts of the British Isles. It's usually a New Year event to scare away evil spirits in the hope of a robust apple harvest in the autumn."

He flung his hand towards the orchard. "As you can see, we're in desperate need of help right now. So we'll use rifles to blast away the ghosties and ghoulies. I do ask that all the children stay well back from the enclosure. Thanks to the traditional flaming torches, the festivities will be visible to all. Also, thanks to the full moon, you might spot the wee spirits flying away in terror."

Laughter rippled through the crowd.

"Now, we'll proceed by tying string with bread around the trees."

He held up a piece of bread dangling by a thread.

"Then we'll pour cider over the bread and the tree roots. To finish, rifles will be fired into the trees whilst others pour on the rest of the cider."

"It's a damn shame to waste such good cider," came a slightly slurred voice from the crowd.

Ignoring the heckler, Callum said, "The cider represents replenishment, whilst the rifles scare away those ghosties in the trees. I hope you all enjoy it, and let's hope it brings about healthy and hearty apples next harvest."

He jumped from the cart and began handing around jugs. Miranda and Ruby passed around the bread already attached to strings.

"Crumbs." I fumbled with the string and bread Ruby handed me. "I can't hold up my ludicrous skirts and help out at the same time. I'd hate to ruin this gown for someone else."

"Let's switch places," said Nurse Kattos. "I'll take the bread for you, and you'll keep an eye on Lady Geraldine."

I couldn't politely say no to this terrifying suggestion. The mere sight of the woman made me flinch.

What would Marie Antoinette do in this situation? Probably tell her servant to stand next to Lady Geraldine. Or she might give Lady Geraldine as good as she got. Yes, that's what I would do.

Lifting my skirts, I carefully trod through the mud to Geraldine's wheelchair.

"Your costume is lovely," I said, focusing on the ingenious red-and-white costume rather than the terrifying lady wearing it. The outfit's clean satin and velvet lines were definitely a Ruby Dove creation. "Have you ever dressed as the Queen of Hearts before?"

"Better than being the Queen of Tarts like you!" She keeled over, rattling with laughter.

Callum bounded over. "Is Auntie all right?"

"Of course I am, child," she snapped. "This lady is quite amusing. Or rather, I'm amusing myself at her expense."

I sighed. At least she was being honest.

"That's all right, then. I'll get back to it."

"Callum is a dear, sweet boy," she said. "He's always been my favourite nephew. Though since his family has vanished, I suppose it's a meaningless statement."

"Do you have children of your own?"

She scowled at me. "Of course not, you stupid tart."

"I am not a tart."

I said the words a bit too loudly. A hush fell over the gathering at precisely the wrong moment. People stared.

Pixley burst into a giggling fit, and everyone soon followed.

He wiped one eye. "No, dear Red, you're not a tart."

Thankfully, a smattering of raindrops distracted the crowd, sending them scurrying to tie the bread-strings around the tree trunks. Mrs Triggs supervised, waving her hands in an officious manner. She'd chatter for a few moments with someone before returning to her position as the official do-gooder of the evening.

Callum announced, "Right. Now it's time for the cider."

Corks popped like fireworks as everyone opened the jugs – except for Callum, Pixley, and Pari, all nattering away about apple wassailing.

Ruby moved nearer to me and winked. She nodded at Lady Geraldine, signalling she was here to eavesdrop but not participate.

Lady Geraldine tugged on my sleeve. "What did you say your name was again?"

"Fina. Fina Aubrey-Havelock."

"It's an unusual name. Italian?"

"Irish. Though a Saint Fina did exist, so you're correct about the Italian version."

"I find it a rather stupid name, regardless of its origin. Callum's wife was named Fina."

My jaw dropped. I left it open, waiting for more.

Lady Geraldine whispered, "We don't speak of Callum's wife. Ever. The tart disappeared with another man, though I heard she died a few months ago. Good riddance to bad rubbish. Mind you, I sensed she was a whore from the beginning, always showing off her bosom like you."

To keep my temper from rising any further, I changed the subject.

"What about Nurse Kattos? How did you find her?"

"Who?"

In a twist of irony, I'd forgotten Lady Geraldine was senile.

"It doesn't matter," I said. "Tell me about your brooch collection."

She quivered, and then her whole body shook. Her eyes closed and her chest heaved.

Nurse Kattos ran to her side. "What happened?"

"I simply asked her about her brooches."

In one swift movement, Nurse Kattos pulled out the leather case I'd noticed yesterday and set it on the apple cider cart. She expertly filled the syringe and jabbed it into Geraldine's arm. The whole procedure took less than a minute.

Soon, Lady Geraldine's body sagged and she stopped shaking.

"Morphine?" I asked.

Nurse Kattos grimaced. "She has these fits, and morphine is the only thing that helps. If I don't catch her in time, she has a seizure."

Callum held his hands to his mouth and boomed, "Time for the main event of the evening."

I whispered to Nurse Kattos, "Should we move Lady Geraldine inside?"

"No. She's fine. The morphine means she can handle anything, and I don't want to miss the rifles."

Callum called, "Will the volunteers come forward?"

Pixley leaned over. "Sounds like they'll need a last cigarette."

"Don't joke about it," said Ruby.

Pari, Miranda, and Milo stepped forward.

"Put a hex on those trees, you witch!" jeered someone from the crowd.

Pari spun around and glared so fiercely it would have silenced even the most determined yapping terrier.

Pari grabbed the rifle from Callum.

My heart stopped, but then I realised she was supposed to fire the rifle.

"I'm glad Pari is aiming her rifle into the trees," murmured Ruby.

Archie yelled from the side-lines, "Daddy! Kill those spirits!"

"Rather a bloodthirsty lot, aren't they?" observed Pixley.

Callum handed a rifle to Milo, and another to Miranda.

Despite knowing nothing about rifles or guns, I surmised Miranda was an expert. She hefted the rifle at a right angle and let it slip through her fingers like butter before twirling it upwards again.

Both Pari and Milo were equally at home with their weapons but had none of the showmanship of Miranda.

Mr Triggs stood near the trio with the firearms, his eyes alight with pleasure. Standing near the dovecote and half-full cider jugs, Mrs Triggs surveyed us indulgently. Next to me, Nurse Kattos stood motionless, whilst Lady Geraldine had her arms crossed and a scowl on her face.

"You don't like guns, do you?" I asked Lady Geraldine.

"No, it's not that. I simply cannot abide the banging racket those rifles make. It's all a ridiculous farce. My nephew is a dear, but he can be a perfect fool sometimes."

Callum leapt up once more onto the cider cart. He gestured to the crowd. "You all have your song sheets. One, two, three …" He waved his hands like a conductor and bellowed in a surprising baritone for someone so small:

"Health to thee, good apple-tree,

Well to bear, pocket-fulls, hat-fulls,

Peck-fulls, bushel-bag-fulls."

A round of rowdy applause met everyone's ears. The boisterous chatter told me everyone had been putting gin in their punch like Pixley.

I held my hand to my head. The gin Pixley had put in my own punch was definitely making me woozy.

But my brain cleared as soon as Callum called, "One, two, and three!"

One gun fired, then another, and then the third. Then for good measure, they did it again.

Wisps of gun smoke rose into the night sky.

In unison, Ruby, Pixley, and I all sighed with relief.

Nurse Kattos leaned over. "You fancied something might go wrong, didn't you?"

I chuckled nervously. "It's silly, but yes."

"Me too." She shivered.

Mrs Triggs held up a tray of glasses. "Time for the last stage! A drink to the trees' health."

"Spiffing," said Pix. "Do you need any assistance, Mrs Triggs?"

She sniffed. "No thank you."

"I've poured cider into these glasses," she continued. "Callum will say a toast and then we'll pour the rest of the cider onto the trees once more."

"Yes, madam," grumbled Pixley.

"Nurse Kattos, will you wake Lady Geraldine?" asked Mrs Triggs.

"She's had a tincture," said Nurse Kattos, as if morphine were simply chamomile tea. "She'll sleep through anything."

We gathered around Mrs Triggs and the tray of glasses, each taking one. The air smelled sweet and spicy. I sniffed my glass, but it smelled only of cider.

Callum raised his glass to the moon.

"She's beautiful tonight, isn't she?" He held a piece of paper aloft and read:

"Here's to thee, old apple-tree,
Whence thou may'st bud, and whence thou may'st blow,
And whence thou may'st bear apples enow
Hats-full! Caps-full!
Bushel-bushel-sacks-full,
And my pockets-full, too, huzza!"

He downed his cider in one go, and we all cried "Huzza" and drank our own, though Milo sipped his carefully.

Callum rubbed his hands. "Right. Now for the last stage. Everyone, pour the rest of the cider onto the trees and bread, please."

The temperature plunged suddenly, so everyone hurriedly sloshed the jugs over the trees, making a satisfying sploshing and gurgling sound.

Then a screeching, shrieking noise came from behind me, like a hawk attacking its prey.

Callum ran to Lady Geraldine, who'd awoken from her stupor. "What is it, Auntie?"

She jabbed a trembling finger at us. "My brooch!"

"Your brooch?" Callum said the words slowly, as if he were processing them equally as slowly.

"She-she-she stole it!" yelled Lady Geraldine, pointing at Mrs Triggs.

I stared at Mrs Triggs's chest. And sure enough, the diamond brooch sparkled in the moonlight.

Mrs Triggs grimaced and clasped her bosom. Then a gurgling, choking sound came from her mouth, and her hands slid to her neck, letting the tray of glasses tumble to the ground.

"I can't, I can't …"

"Beryl!" Mr Triggs held his wife's arm, trying to hold her steady.

But it was no use.

Beryl Triggs flopped backwards onto the grass, her eyes wide open, staring glassily at the moon.

CHAPTER
Eight

"DRINK THIS." I handed Ruby a brimming glass of sherry.

She sipped it and grimaced. "It's absolutely vile, Feens. How about brandy?"

Pixley grabbed Ruby's glass and downed the sherry in one go. "Keep them coming," he said. "Must keep out the chill."

Callum strode into the chaotic kitchen, running his hands through his floppy hair. "Right. The police are questioning the others."

"Did the other guests go home?" asked Ruby.

"No. I asked everyone to stay and to report to the police."

Pixley swung one leg on a chair and hitched up his trouser leg. "Why did you telephone the police? Do you suspect foul play?"

Callum scanned the room, clearly avoiding my gaze.

"First, Aunt Geraldine's brooch disappears," Callum said. "And then Mrs Triggs keels over dead? With the brooch pinned to her lapel?"

"I see," said Pixley. "When you put it that way, it does sound peculiar."

"Surely she died of a heart attack," I said. "The shock of being accused of stealing the brooch must have brought on the attack.

Mrs Triggs obviously cared about her social standing – she must have been absolutely mortified."

This time, Callum had no trouble staring at me. "You would say that, wouldn't you?"

Ruby coughed. "Callum is right, Feens. Something wasn't right, but I can't put my finger on it."

"No need, Miss Dove. The police will arrive soon." Callum left the room.

I glared at Ruby. "Thanks for putting me in the soup, Ruby."

Her eyes widened. "What do you mean?"

"Yes, do tell us," said Pixley. "And what did Callum mean by 'you would say that'?"

As a stampede of footsteps echoed in the corridor, I realised Ruby and Pixley weren't aware that Callum suspected me of pinching Lady Geraldine's brooch.

But it was too late to tell them. The police had arrived.

With pursed lips, Callum said, "This is Inspector Alfreda Whittle and Sergeant Sheridan Ainsley from the Oxfordshire Police."

"Thank you, Mr Sinclair. It's actually *Chief* Inspector Whittle," said a woman's voice with a northern accent.

I looked up. My brandy glass slid from my hands. In one fluid movement, Pixley caught the glass before it hit the marble floor.

Ruby's glass also slid to the floor, but Pixley wasn't quick enough to catch hers.

Within a second of the glass smashing, the woman said, "Sergeant, see to the mess."

"Right away, ma'am," said the sergeant, in a cut-glass accent.

Chief Inspector Whittle was a woman. I'd heard of a woman becoming a chief inspector a few years ago, but I'd never witnessed it. And whilst I admired her, I still surveyed her critically. After all, she was a rozzer.

A double-breasted topcoat completely swallowed Whittle's quite short and stocky frame, recalling one of the immovable tree trunks from the orchard outside. And her pink, ruddy face suggested a farming life rather than one in the police force. But her ebullient eyes sparkled like a magpie's surveying a scene strewn with scavenged food.

Pixley strode forward, arm outstretched. "Pixley Hayford, the *Daily Rumble*."

Her eyes crinkled at the corners. "A journalist, are you? How convenient."

What did she mean by that?

She turned towards us. "And I hear you two are Oxford students."

We nodded in unison. I said, "Yes, madam. Sorry. Chief Inspector."

"And what can you tell us about tonight?"

Ruby opened her mouth to speak, but Callum put in, "Sorry to interrupt, but Miss Aubrey-Havelock ought to tell us her story first."

I winced, my mind whirring through the night's events like a film. The gin made this considerably more difficult, blending pictures and blurring the timeline.

With a halting breath, I recounted my adventures from the moment that effing witch soiled my Robin Hood outfit up until the lights went out. I didn't mention my encounter with the mysterious skeleton, mostly because it seemed positively barmy, but also because it might raise more suspicions about the blasted brooch disappearance.

I tripped over my last words, my mind suddenly recalling the piece of paper I'd hidden in my bosom. Perhaps I should excuse myself to read it.

With an abrupt halt I asked, "May I use the toilet?"

Whittle's eyebrows rose, but the surprise was momentary. "Of course. Just as soon as we clear up a little matter. Right, Sergeant Ainsley?"

"Quite right, ma'am." He flipped through his notebook,

sucking on his pencil. Sergeant Ainsley was the definition of a blue-eyed boy: tall with slightly tousled blond hair, a lean, square face, and an affable manner hiding extreme entitlement. Surely he wasn't obliged to work at all. So why was he working in the police force?

With one graceful movement, Ainsley closed his notebook. "And that is the matter of the brooch. Did you recognise it when you spotted it on the deceased?"

"No, how would I?" I asked. "Whomever stole the brooch took it before I was in Lady Geraldine's room searching for my costume."

"What are your theories about the mysterious disappearance and reappearance of this brooch?"

"What do you mean, 'theories'? Isn't it obvious that Mrs Triggs pinched it herself?"

"But why would she display the brooch in front of all those people?" Ainsley asked. "Not least of all Lady Geraldine herself?"

"Haven't the foggiest," I said. "That's your job."

A smirk marred the sergeant's beautiful face.

"Miss Aubrey-Havelock," said Whittle, "you're quite right that it's our job. Now, why don't you find the smallest room whilst I chat with your friends?"

I was relieved but also puzzled.

"Are you sure?" I asked.

"Oh, go on with you," she said.

I left the room, still puzzled. Chief Inspector Whittle was disarmingly charming, like your favourite aunt who gives you an extra biscuit when no one is looking. Every other police officer we'd met would not have let my unwisely flippant comment go unnoted. But she did.

I hung back in the corridor, eavesdropping on what Ruby and Pixley had to say.

"Now, Miss Dove," said Whittle. "Did you observe anything unusual or unexpected during the apple howling?"

"Not particularly," said Ruby. "But it was a new experience, so I'm not certain what 'unexpected' means."

Ruby Dove was a good egg. Playing for time.

"Anything that made you think 'Well, that's peculiar'?"

"I'm afraid I was fixated on the rifles. I don't like guns, and the set-up made me nervous," said Ruby.

"Why did you participate, then?"

"Community spirit, I suppose. I helped out with the fancy dress designs, and Callum invited us."

"Did Mr Sinclair invite you specifically?"

"No, it was a general invite to everyone in the village who'd helped with the festivities."

"I see. But I understand Mr Hayford here is from London. How was he involved?"

Pixley piped up, "Ruby and Fina are chums, Chief Inspector. They wanted a third wheel, so I'm always happy to oblige them. Besides, I'm always on the prowl for a scoop."

"Most accommodating of you," Whittle said with a tinge of sarcasm. "Now, as you're aware, both the sergeant and I investigate suspicious deaths. Do either of you suspect foul play, as does Mr Sinclair?"

I shifted my position closer to the door. Around the corner, I spied the two of them shaking their heads.

"So, you believe Mrs Triggs stole Lady Geraldine's brooch, then pinned it to her lapel and went about organising the festivities as if nothing had happened? Then she dropped dead when she was accused of stealing it?"

"It does sound barmy," Pixley said.

"Barmy is the word, Mr Hayford," Whittle said. "Can you think of any explanation? Either of you?"

"Perhaps she was a kleptomaniac?" put in Ruby.

"I thought Oxford students were brighter than that. My sergeant here took his degree there, and he'd never suggest such a thing, would you?"

"No, ma'am," said Ainsley. "My psychology tutor did discuss kleptomania, but not cases involving a purposeful display of the stolen goods."

"My apologies to Oxford University for my mental dullness," Ruby said, with a bitterness only Pixley and I would notice.

"What do you think of Mr Sinclair?" Whittle asked.

"Mr Sinclair?" Ruby sounded surprised. "Why?"

"If you'd just answer the question, Miss Dove." Whittle sounded perturbed.

"I cannot say I've known him long enough to have an opinion."

"Do you know anything about his antecedents? Reasons for coming down from Scotland?"

"To take care of his aunt. At least that's what we surmised."

Whittle sniffed, clearly unconvinced. I supposed the chief inspector's scepticism about Callum was warranted. After all, it was his party, his house, and it was his aunt's brooch. Though I hadn't the foggiest how it all tied together with Beryl Triggs.

But I was satisfied that my friends had the police well in hand, so I crept down the corridor to the toilet. Since the scrap of paper was stowed in my bodice, I wasn't keen to undress in public.

As I passed the conservatory, Milo's flat, nasal voice floated from the room. Try as he might, his whisper was anything but quiet.

Then I heard Miranda's voice.

"Milo, I can't keep doing this. You know it's wrong. What if Pari finds out?"

"Forget about Pari. What if the police find out?"

"They won't. Besides, Beryl died of natural causes."

"If she didn't, it was probably Nigel who did it."

"Why? They were devoted to each other."

"Do you really believe that?"

Footsteps approached, so I scampered to the loo.

I locked the door and hoped the paper hadn't slid out during all the excitement.

Someone tapped on the door.

"Yes, what is it?"

It was Callum. "The police wish to speak with you."

"Well, as I told them," I said with rising irritation, "I had to use the loo. And that's what I'm doing. Would it be too much to ask for a minute of peace?"

Really, the man was too persistent. After all, it was only a blasted brooch. Valuable, yes, but Lady Geraldine had oodles of them. Mrs Triggs might have been so repressed by all those good works that she simply had a moment of madness when she pinched the brooch. I couldn't blame her, after being buried down here in Crickle Hythe.

And murder seemed a preposterous suggestion. Besides, how would the murderer have done it? Maybe Lady Geraldine had a poison dart hidden in her wheelchair which she threw at Mrs Triggs? Absolute tosh.

After another moment, Callum's footsteps faded away.

I unbuttoned my top and the paper fell to the floor, but there was no need to pick it up. It screamed back at me: "YOU ARE BEING WATCHED".

My heart didn't just thump, it positively thundered.

More footsteps.

With a sharp jerk on the chain, I flushed the paper down the loo. It might be police evidence, but I certainly wasn't going to share it with them.

Making my way back down the corridor, I heard Chief Inspector Whittle's voice in the conservatory. She was discussing why Scotland Yard wouldn't be called in on the case. If it were a case of murder at all.

Then I heard Nigel say, "Miss Aubrey-Havelock told me not to say anything about the brooch vanishing."

"Did she now?" came Whittle's voice.

"Aye, that girl is wrapped up in this somehow," said Callum.

"Yes, Mr Sinclair, I must agree with you. We'll be detaining Miss Aubrey-Havelock for further questioning."

Whittle sniffed. "Sergeant Ainsley, please locate Miss Aubrey-Havelock. I'm beginning to doubt she'll ever return from the toilet."

So I picked up my skirts, kicked off my heels, dashed through the kitchen, and escaped into the milky moonlight.

CHAPTER
Nine

HALFWAY TO RUBY'S COTTAGE, I stopped, struggling to take a decision.

In the first moments of running from Chidden Park, my scrambled mind had planned to take supplies from Ruby's cottage before hiding somewhere. Where? In the woods? That plan seemed foolhardy now. And hiding in Pixley's narrowboat was a daft idea since the police would undoubtedly search there.

The moon cast a blue shadow on the calmly rippling water. Without the precious moonlight, I surely would have tumbled into the canal by now. And my poor Marie Antoinette gown had already gone the way of haughty Marie herself: finished for good. Not to mention my freezing and wet toes, only covered by stockings and mud.

I stared at gauzy, moonlit clouds, hoping they would spark a brainwave. Perhaps I could howl at them.

Focus, Fina, focus.

Right. Ruby and Pixley would try to throw the police off my scent, which also meant I had to stay away from them. I considered a bus or train – any would do – but the police would be watching the local stations. Besides, my get-up ensured everyone would remember me.

An owl hooted, drawing my eyes back to Thrupp Woods. I could hide amongst the trees, but for how long? Police dogs would find me, and again, in this yellow-and-white gown, I'd be easily spotted.

No, my hideout required shelter. A cottage. Maybe a village cottage? I squeezed my eyes shut, painting a mental map of Crickle Hythe's lanes.

The high street featured Milo's Drowned Duck pub, the Triggses' village stores, and Miranda Oliver's chemist. And at the far end of the high street sat Pari's garage.

I snapped my fingers. Of course! I'd hide in Pari's garage, somewhere the police would never search.

After winding my way behind the high street along deserted lanes, I soon spotted a green sign in gold lettering, which read "Karan's Garage". I edged along the side of the building, my hand groping the wall, away from the blackberry bushes reaching for my silken gown. The pathway around the back smelled of petrol and rotting leaves.

A few pushes against the first rickety wooden door led nowhere. Around the back, a double door was fastened shut with a thick, shiny lock. Next to the door stood a chair with a damp, sooty ashtray.

I set the ashtray on the ground and lifted the chair. If I hit the lock at the right angle, it would break open. Lifting my arms above my head, I thrust the chair down on the silver metal.

Well, it had worked in films.

I tried again. And again.

In my increasing frenzy, I'd failed to notice the hum of a motor car in the lane. Now it made itself known with a loud roar of its engine.

I dropped the chair and peeked around the corner. Headlamps glowed in the darkness like ski tracks on fresh snow.

"Maybe she went in here, guv," came a voice.

"Nah, not in that get-up," said an older, raspy voice. "She probably hopped on a train to London to one of her toff friends."

Forgetting I was hiding from the police, I let out a snort of indignation.

"Did you hear something?" said the first voice.

"It was a pig, George, or some type of rodent vermin. Maybe a badger?"

"Are badgers rodents, guv? And do they snort?"

"Dunno. But ladies don't."

I clasped my mouth and nose to suppress yet another lady-like snort.

The engine revved, and I lifted the chair once more, sure that this time the lock would break.

But then the engine stopped again.

The older one said, "Like a hog, I'd better follow my nose. Something tells me there's someone around the back."

George said, "Maybe it's a tramp, guv."

"Maybe. But it always pays to look, it always pays to look."

My blood pulsed so hard that my teeth hurt. Damn and blast it. My head spun, searching for somewhere to hide, but everything was covered in bracken and dead leaves.

Torchlight played against the sky like a West End spectacle, moving closer to me.

Frozen on the spot, my body simply wouldn't move. All my senses were alive to the smell of the earth, the tiny sliver of wind at my neck, and the blue-black of my surroundings.

A shaft of moonlight suddenly lit up the padlock. The beauty was unlocked! Either the lock had been open since the very beginning, or my little trick learnt from the cinema had worked.

Yanking the lock, I twisted it down and away from the door. I slid in through the crack, not wanting to jam it on the tufts of grass should I open the door too far.

Police torchlight still streamed in through the slats in the wood, so I crouched behind the door, sinking into a small puddle of petrol.

And although my blood was already running cold, my whole

body went numb when I heard the next noise coming from outside: the crack of a match being lit.

I held my breath and squeezed my eyes shut, completely unprepared to meet my so-called maker. Though my life had been short, it certainly had its moments. My grandmother would say I should be grateful for that.

"Oi!" called the older policeman. "What are you like, George? Are you mad? Put that out!"

"Sorry, guv. Just wanted a smoke."

"Well, that's exactly what we'll become if you light up. There's petrol about, remember? You'll get us blown sky-high."

The smell of tobacco vanished, and my breathing resumed its usual rhythm. Though my arms and legs were still frozen with adrenaline.

"Sorry, guv." Pause. "Should we go? No one's here."

The guv'nor groaned. "Look here!"

I stiffened, moving closer to the wall. Now in a complete foetal position, I couldn't possibly make myself any smaller.

"There's footprints, and they're very small."

"But they don't look like ladies' shoes, guv."

"She's probably barefoot by now if she's been running through the countryside."

"The footprints go into the woods but then they stop, guv."

"All right. We can't search in there on our own. The lads at Chidden Park are organising a search of the woods."

"Why are they so keen on catching her? Do they reckon she did the murder?"

"Chief Inspector Whittle is keen on this Havelock girl as her prime suspect. And since Her Ladyship or what have you did a runner, she must be the killer."

"But didn't Mrs Triggs die of a fit? Or a heart attack?"

"The lord of the manor doesn't think so."

A motor car rumbled in the distance.

With a sharp intake of breath, the policeman said, "That'll be Whittle now."

CHAPTER
Ten

THE NEXT MORNING, I awoke smelling petrol and, strangely enough, stale cigarettes. Despite being cold, wet, and stiff, I lay on my back, blinking into the darkness. A weak daylight streamed through tiny gaps in the roof, and energetic songbirds were determined to usher me into a better day.

Not bloody likely.

Luckily, the arrival of Chief Inspector Whittle's car the night before had been the sign for my tormentors to leave. One blessing of complete exhaustion was the ability to sleep in any position and in anything, or in this case, a puddle of petrol.

Prying my stiff arms apart and lengthening my legs, I rose like an old woman with rheumatism.

I was ravenous, thirsty, and confused. I couldn't stay here – at least not for long. And I'd need a change of clothes, especially since these blasted skirts were impossible to walk in, let alone run.

Spotting some grey overalls on a hook, I made a quick change from my soiled togs into the decidedly stiff full-body mechanic's uniform. At least I was dry now and could walk if I spread my legs apart like a wind-up toy.

"Are you Mummy's new mechanic?" squeaked a voice behind me.

I spun round.

It was the pink-and-purple fairy I'd seen upstairs at the gala the night before. Though she was in her normal clothes, the same two pigtails brushed her shoulders – her one concession to the frivolousness of childhood. Otherwise, she was twelve going on thirty.

"I'm Clorinda," I said, using the first name that came into my head. I have a cousin named Clorinda.

"Clorinda," the fairy said flatly.

Selkies and kelpies, I couldn't even convince a twelve-year-old. On the other hand, children were the best at seeing right through lies, weren't they?

"What's your name?" I asked.

"Ethylene. But everyone calls me Etty."

"Ethylene?" I said, trying to recall why it was familiar.

With a very adult stretching of her fingers, Etty said, "Yes, Ethylene is also the name of a chemical, but the girls' name is much older. It's a Celtic word for 'noble'. Mummy says my silly daddy insisted on the name. But we don't talk about him since he's gone."

"Well, Etty, run along now whilst I get to work."

"You don't look like a mechanic."

"And you don't look like a fairy. Or a chemical for that matter. Now, run along."

She shrugged. "You'll see."

I rubbed my eyes. I wouldn't have normally been so abrupt with Etty, but I was short on sleep, and more importantly, food.

Food. Among the heaps of receipts and notes scattered across a shelf, I spotted a brown paper package that must be a sandwich. Unwrapping it revealed wilted greenery and a limp slice of cheese between two hard slices of bread. No matter, it was sustenance. I chomped away greedily, nearly missing the sound of yet another car in the distance.

After it had halted in front of the garage, I heard Etty speaking to someone as if she, Etty, were the owner of the business.

The other voice came closer. It sounded like Miranda Oliver, and she was headed my way.

With a great gulp, I finished my sandwich and stuffed the paper into my uniform. I scanned the room for another hiding place. Unlike the rear of the garage, the front was quite tidy and open. Then I spotted the little trolley-tray mechanics use to slide under motor cars. It was my only chance to hide.

I lowered myself onto the trolley and shot underneath the nearest car. It was the perfect hiding place, except for one thing. The oily smell of petrol clogged my nostrils, and the mechanical innards of the car sat inches from my nose. Claustrophobia. I'd had this sensation only once before, when my brother shut me in a broom closet in a rather extreme childhood game of Sardines.

Breathe, Fina, breathe.

Squeezing my eyes shut, I concentrated on the voice that was sure to come.

"Hullo. Etty tells me your name is Clorinda. I'm Miranda Oliver, a friend of Pari's."

Should I lower my vocal pitch or heighten it?

Opting for a lowered voice, I said, "Pleased to meet you. Be out in a minute."

"That's all right. I was looking for Pari to tell her the news."

"News?" I said, knowing full well she meant the murder, or rather, the death by natural causes, as I was convinced it was.

"Yes. They've arrested that girl."

"Ow!" I cried, banging my head on the bottom of the car. My involuntary rocking motion upwards not only hit my head against the chassis, but it sent me off balance. Slowly, I rolled out from underneath the car.

"Jeepers!" Miranda cried. "You're Fina. The one who vanished!"

I ignored her exclamations. "Yes, yes, yes. Just tell me one thing. Which girl have they arrested?"

Pari wrapped me in a blanket and shoved a mug of hot tea into my hands.

"Drink," she ordered.

Gladly following instructions, I downed the tea. Seeing me splutter as the tea came through my nose, Pari slapped me on the back.

"A little Scotch for what ails you," she said.

"Good grief." I caught my breath. "I mean, thank you." My muscles warmed and loosened from the alcohol.

Pari moved to the kitchen sink and began the washing-up, giving me ample time to survey her cottage. Dried herbs hung from the ceiling, and a cauldron boiled on a grate in the fireplace. A hotchpotch of blue and green bottles lined the windowsills, and a black cat sat hunched in the corner, flicking its tail.

Perhaps I had taken the cat's seat.

Before I could stop myself, I asked, "Are you a witch?"

The dishes clattered in the sink. Pari wiped her brow with her forearm and gave a forced chuckle. "No, but it does resemble a witch's cottage, doesn't it?"

She leaned against the counter. "As you might know, Miranda is the village chemist. People travel from as far as Scotland to come to her shop. She has an interest in herbs and homeopathy, so she started decorating her ultra-modern cottage like this. But then village busybodies began whispering she was a witch. So, she moved all of her herbs and potions here."

"I see."

Pari shook her black curls. "I wonder if you do."

The room had been quiet before, but now it became close, as if someone had sealed a jam jar shut.

Time to change the subject. "I expect you're curious about that get-up I was wearing in your garage."

Pari wiped a dish dry. "Now you mention it, I was intrigued. Damned incomers like you always create havoc."

"I'm not an incomer." I slammed my teacup on the table.

"Yes you are."

"Right. Well. Sort of. In any case, I ran from the police last night because they were going to arrest me."

"So you did kill Beryl Triggs. Well done. Good riddance to bad rubbish, I say."

Pari was a remarkable woman. She said what she thought – much like I did – but she didn't blurt it out or feel ashamed of it.

"You're not a hypocrite, are you?" I asked.

"I'm a damned grumpy mechanic. But no, I try not to be a hypocrite."

The bell rang and I soon heard Etty's voice trilling as she opened the door.

Etty floated in, followed by purposeful, marching steps behind her.

"Good morning, Milo," said Pari. "Look who turned up underneath a car this morning."

Milo was dressed in tight-fitting trousers and jacket. And his shirt was unbuttoned one button too many.

I lifted my mug in a weak salute. "It was the only place I could hide from the police. And before you ask, no, I did not kill Beryl Triggs. And I still don't think she was murdered."

"Well, the police disagree with you," he said. "They've arrested your friend Ruby."

My stomach tightened again at the reminder of what had happened to Ruby. Every time I tried to formulate a question about her, my throat closed and my mouth ran dry.

Milo turned to Pari. "Have you seen Miranda?"

Pari sniffed and waved a tea towel at me. "Miranda brought this poor creature here this morning and then toddled off to work. Isn't she at the chemist's?"

Milo wiped his eye with a forefinger. "No, she wasn't there, so I tried the village stores. Nigel is positively mad. I can't believe he opened the shop this morning."

Pari crossed her arms. "Why are you looking for Miranda?"

Even in my addled state I sensed the tension between these two.

As if he were upping the ante, Milo also crossed his arms, biceps flexing. "Miranda was helping me with a cocktail recipe."

Pari's arms didn't budge. "You run a pub, Milo. I'm aware you're from Toronto, but the denizens of Crickle Hythe don't partake in posh drinks."

"I'm from Ottawa, actually. But never mind that. And you'd be surprised at the people we get coming through the pub these days."

Pari snorted. "More incomers."

"Crickle Hythe is near Oxford. It will always have incomers."

For a moment, I thought Pari might reach out and strangle Milo's thick neck. Instead, she cocked her head. "Crickle Hythe is a refuge for eccentrics escaping Oxford. Like me. Like Miranda. We both were sent down."

"I know. I'm an escapee, too. Though from the air force, not Oxford."

"I remember." Pari let her arms drop. "Look here, I haven't a clue where Miranda is, but I'm confident she'll turn up. Now, if you don't mind, I must see to our little waif and stray here before going to work."

Milo twisted the ring on his hand. "I was sorry to hear about your friend, Miss Aubrey-Havelock. But that chief inspector woman said they're rushing the autopsy, so maybe they'll let her go then."

"Why did they arrest Ruby? On what evidence?" I asked.

Pari grimaced at Milo. He bit his lip. "Ah. Yes, you wouldn't have heard. She gave herself up. Miss Dove admitted to killing Mrs Triggs."

Up until now, my mind hadn't taken in everything. I stared up at the herbs suddenly swimming before my eyes like stalactites hanging from the ceiling. I stumbled to my feet.

"I must go. I must go and find Ruby." I rubbed my forehead. "No. I must find Pixley. Yes, Pixley will know what to do."

Etty traipsed in. "Mummy, what's wrong with Clorinda?"

"Her name's Fina, sweetie. And I think she's had a shock."

CHAPTER
Eleven

A FEW HOURS LATER, I jerked awake in a bed piled high with blankets. I blinked, my surroundings soon returning me to reality. A surreal reality, to be sure. But the soup aromas and the tinny voice of Etty singing downstairs told me I was still in Pari's cottage.

My stomach rumbled, upset with me for depriving it of food for so long. As I liked to remind Ruby, a little snack every two hours kept the old gastric juices flowing, and me happy.

Remembering the stale sandwich I'd found at the garage, I reached for the uniform on the chair. Perhaps a bit was left over.

The brown paper only contained crumbs, but I noticed for the first time that it also had typeface on the back.

I smoothed it flat on the side table. It was a notice about an upcoming local council meeting. I wouldn't have given it a second thought, except for the red circle drawn around the agenda: canal regulations, a proposed development, and a village fête.

My curiosity was aroused, and the old grey cells – or rather, grey mush – finally tripped into gear. I must find Pixley. Between the two of us, we'd solve this murder case and Ruby would be freed. If it was really a murder at all.

But first things first. I was wearing a voluminous nightie,

undoubtedly one of Pari's floaty pieces of nonsense. Where were my shoes? I peeked under the bed.

I heard footfall on the stairs, so I righted myself, but fell back into the pillows, nearly fainting after the rush of blood to my head.

"Aha! The escapee princess has been found!" chirped Pixley in the doorway.

"I was Marie Antoinette, not a princess," I said sourly. I ought to have been overjoyed to see Pixley, but his appearance had only provoked a strange resentment.

"What's eating you, Red? Not enough sleep?" He put a finger to his cheek and twisted it, as if he were an innocent new-born babe. "Aha! The great Pixley Holmes has deduced that you have not been fed on the regular. Time to put on the old nosebag."

A plate of sandwiches materialised from behind his back. "Voilà!"

I exhaled, my resentment draining away.

As I chomped my delicious cheese sandwich, Pixley made himself at home. "Comfortable cottage, what? A real museum piece. And that Pari is most hospitable once you move past her alarming façade."

"Mmph."

"That's right. You eat, I'll talk." He laid one foot casually across his knee. "Now, the intrepid Sherlock Dove – no, make that Ruby Holmes – confessed to the murder after you fled the scene of the crime. Before that, I believe the entire police force of Oxfordshire were searching for a bedraggled princess in yellow and white."

"I was Marie Antoinette," I mumbled through the crumbs.

"Whatever. I never cared for headless Marie, though I do enjoy a spot of cake with my tea. In any case, Ruby gave herself up to old Whittle."

"But why?"

"To protect you."

"Was I in danger?"

"Not exactly, but Ruby knew if they found you, they'd definitely speed up the process of charging you. You know how the police are – if you scarper, it's as good as admitting to the crime."

"Chief Inspector Whittle struck me as brighter than that."

He swiped a sandwich and neatly stuffed it into his mouth. "True. Old Whittle is definitely one to watch. Ruby said so last night. And that smarmy blue-eyed Aryan sidekick."

"Don't joke about Aryans."

"I'm not! I mean it. There's something too clean about that bloke."

"Well, he's the least of our troubles," I said, then launched into a recounting of everything I'd heard and seen the night before.

"That message from the skeleton in Lady Geraldine's room is deuced disturbing," said Pixley. "Was it a warning or a threat?"

"Either way, we must be on our guard."

He slapped his knee and stood up. "The time has come, my friend. We can't avoid a chinwag with our friend Whittle any longer."

———

Pixley and I ambled along Crickle Hythe's high street past the chemist, where a cheerful "Closed" sign hung in the window. It was a stylish shop, like the owner, full of gleaming chrome and every shade of red.

Though Crickle Hythe was tiny, it boasted a delightful village green: a roundish patch of emerald set off by a tea-coloured pond. A row of hunched thatched cottages sat as if they were queuing to enter the Drowned Duck across the lane. At the other end sat a sadly vacant tea shop, next to the village stores. Ruby had said the owner had tired of English winters so she'd sold up and retired to the south of France.

Pixley pointed at the eyebrow windows of the pub. "Milo told me that when he bought the Duck, the first thing he asked the elderly owner was about the unusual name. Apparently, she'd kept a pen of ducks near her cottage on the other side of the pub. One day, she'd returned home to find ducks strewn about her garden, all dead. True to her efficient spirit, she had a good cry for five minutes and then got busy plucking them for the pot."

I shivered. "A bit too efficient for my taste."

He waved my interruption aside. "Within an hour of her plucking them, they suddenly came back to life, sliding off the counter and quacking at her angrily. When she inspected the garden, she spotted a hole in the fence where a dripping keg of bitter had formed a pool of beer. The poor duckies had all been dead drunk. Of course, they were all naked since she'd plucked them, so the owner knitted them tiny jumpers and renamed her pub the Drowned Duck."

The Drowned Duck dominated the green, sprawling across one full corner of it. This was relative, as all the other buildings on the green were so small – including Crickle Hythe Village Stores, which was doing a busy trade on this overcast morning. Mr Triggs must be a man who dealt with grief by simply carrying on.

As we circled the village green, Sergeant Ainsley burst from the pub.

"Miss Aubrey-Havelock!"

"That's my name, Sergeant," I said, feeling an unusual wave of calm wash over me.

"The police have been searching for you."

I crossed my arms. "What of it? And why? Didn't Ruby confess to the crime?" Even as I uttered the words, I felt disloyal to her.

Ainsley's jaw pulsed. "You could be charged, you know."

Holding out my wrists, I said, "Well, go on, then."

"Leave it, Ainsley." Chief Inspector Whittle reached up and tousled his hair.

The sergeant flinched, but didn't react.

With this one simple gesture, Chief Inspector Whittle had suddenly become my favourite copper.

Whittle jerked her head towards the pub. "Why don't you two join us inside?"

Whilst I was grateful to avoid taking the bus to Oxford Police Station, my legs tensed at the thought of being questioned.

"Come on, Red." Pixley lightly touched my back. "You're an old hand at this by now. Don't let them intimidate you."

"You're right, Pix."

Unlike the Duck's sprawling exterior, the inside was neatly divided into the public bar, a snug, a taproom, and a meeting room in the back. Tarnished horse brasses lined the open fireplace. Mismatched comfortable chairs were scattered about, and the bar itself had a counter that looked as old as the pub, scored and dented from generations of drinkers.

On a bench near the front window, a miniature schnauzer lifted its head. It peered at us in that permanently grumpy way that schnauzers do, and then let its head drop, keeping one watchful eye on us.

Milo was wiping the bar. He stopped, throwing the rag over his shoulder and striding towards us with a slight swagger in his step.

"What'll you have?" he asked.

"A bitter for me," said Pixley.

"Just bring us a pot of tea and three cups," said Whittle.

I wasn't going to object to tea. Though the dulling effect of alcohol would have been welcome at that moment, I needed what few wits I still had.

After a few minutes, Milo brought our drinks and Whittle lowered herself into a chair. She leaned back. "We could charge you after your little escapade last night, Miss Aubrey-Havelock."

I stuck out my chin. "Well?"

"Out of curiosity, where did you spend the night?"

"In the woods," I said defiantly.

She grimaced at her tea, as if it were too hot. "I see. Well, let's leave that aside for the moment. Tell us, why did you run away in the first place?"

"I've dealt with the police before, so I when I overheard you planning to arrest me, I wasn't going to wait around."

Pixley shifted in his chair.

I'd put my foot in it. Again.

"You've dealt with the police before." A tiny smirk played across Whittle's face. "Tell us more."

"I meant the Cutmere Perch incident in Cornwall, which you must have read about in the papers."

"Ah, yes. The murderer who disappeared into the Atlantic."

"Quite."

"Well, we have information that might surprise you."

"About Cutmere Perch?"

She exchanged a glance with Ainsley. So there *was* something.

"No, not about Cutmere Perch. About Mrs Beryl Triggs's untimely demise."

She lifted her chin in Pixley's direction. "Before I say anything, let me make it perfectly clear that I'll charge you with obstruction, Mr Hayford, if you write a story about this."

"Mum's the word, Chief Inspector," he said.

"It's obviously too soon for the autopsy, but the pathologist gave me a preliminary report. Though he said it was too soon to confirm it's murder, she probably died from cyanide poisoning."

CHAPTER
Twelve

PIXLEY LET OUT A LOW WHISTLE.

At the bar, Milo quietly flapped his rag on the counter. After a moment's hesitation, he approached us.

"Sorry to butt in like this, Chief Inspector. But I hope you don't mind if I join you, seeing as I was at the gala last night."

"Take a pew, Mr Judson," Whittle said. "We'll have to question you again in any case, so you'll save us time by joining in."

At the sight of Milo sitting, the schnauzer leapt off the bench and trotted towards us.

"Come on, Bertie." Milo patted the seat next to him. Bertie leapt onto the chair and rolled onto his back, paws in the air. Milo scratched his belly. Despite his grumpy colouring, I swore Bertie was smiling at me.

At least someone was enjoying himself.

"Did you find any evidence of cyanide?" asked Pixley. "I mean, did she eat it? Or drink it?"

Ainsley riffled through his notebook. "We don't have the official report yet, but it does appear that one of the glasses on the tray of cider had cyanide residue."

"What about the cider jugs?" I asked.

"One of those also contained cyanide. We also dusted for

fingerprints, but it proves nothing because one can easily slip cyanide into a jug without holding it."

Milo rubbed Bertie's chin. "So someone put cyanide in the cider jug. Then it was poured into the glasses and poor Mrs Triggs drank it."

Did Milo actually believe she was "poor" Mrs Triggs? He had different opinions last night, but I wouldn't share that with the police.

Pixley held up a finger. "Half a mo, that doesn't make sense. If the cyanide was in the jug, why would it be in only *one* of the glasses? Wouldn't it be in all of them?" He shivered. "To put it plainly, why aren't we all dead?"

"Excellent point, Mr Hayford," said Whittle. "But we asked Mr Judson about that earlier and he recollects that the glasses were filled by two jugs. A bit was left in one jug, presumably what was used to fill Mrs Triggs's glass. The unadulterated full jug was used to fill everyone else's glasses."

"Rather convenient, that," said Pixley.

"I agree," said Whittle. "How could the murderer plan that so carefully?"

"And how could the murderer be certain Mrs Triggs would take the poisoned cider glass?" I asked.

Everyone nodded.

Whittle ran a finger across her eyebrow. "It's all too coincidental and haphazard."

Pixley turned to me. "Fina has the most marvellous memory. Do you remember what happened?"

I closed my eyes and let the picture flash before me. "Pari, Nigel, and Milo unloaded the cider jugs from the cart. Then Miranda and Ruby handed round that bread tied to a string. Callum handed out the jugs."

"Were the jugs open then?" asked Whittle.

"No, they were all sealed. You'd notice anyone opening them because they made a popping sound." I paused. "Then, because I was having trouble tying the string because of my long skirts, I took Nurse Kattos's place next to Lady Geraldine."

"Yes, I remember you switching places," said Pixley.

"Then everyone opened the jugs and poured the cider over the bread on the trees and the tree roots, as instructed."

"Everyone?" asked Ainsley.

With my eyes still closed, I said, "Pari, Pixley, and Callum didn't participate in pouring of the cider."

Pixley coughed. "I was chatting with them about the apple-howling tradition. Thought I might write it up as a story."

"Then Lady Geraldine had a convulsive fit and Nurse Kattos injected her with morphine," I said.

"Are you certain that was all Nurse Kattos had?" asked Whittle. "Were there other vials in her bag?"

"If you mean a vial of cyanide, I didn't notice any, but that's because it was one of those single syringe kits – not an entire bag."

"Go on," Whittle said. "So Nurse Kattos injected Lady Geraldine."

"And then Miranda, Pari, and Milo took their places with the rifles."

Ainsley said, "At this point, where were the jugs? Could anyone be tampering with them?"

"The jugs all sat next to Mrs Triggs, so she would have noticed any funny business," said Milo. "And that's a risk I'd never take with Beryl Triggs – she noticed everything."

"I agree with Milo about the jugs," I said. Still with my eyes closed, I carried on. "Back to the rifles. It seemed peculiar that Miranda was so at ease with the rifle."

"I'll say," said Milo. "Seemed like she was a marksman."

"After Callum read the poem," I continued, "they fired the rifles. Following that was Callum's toast."

Whittle chewed her pencil. "Now we come to the key point: was Mrs Triggs the only one to pour cider into the glasses?"

"Absolutely," I said.

"How can you be so confident?" asked Ainsley.

"Like Ruby, I'm not fond of guns. Instead, I focused on what everyone was doing instead of the event itself."

"So this means that Mrs Triggs either committed suicide in a very peculiar way," said Pixley, "or she meant to murder someone else but accidentally drank from the wrong glass."

"Neither of which is plausible," said Whittle with finality. "Continue, Miss Aubrey-Havelock."

"In preparation for the toast, we all took glasses from the same tray. The murderer could not have slipped cyanide into a glass because we were all staring at the tray. Then we all gulped down our cider, though I remember Milo sipping his."

"Not a fan of the cider, that's why," Milo said. "But I did drink half before placing it back on the tray."

"After we finished the cider," I said, "everyone emptied the jugs onto the bread and trees again. And I mean everyone except myself and Lady Geraldine. Then they loaded the cart with the empty jugs."

"But Lady Geraldine interrupted that," said Milo.

"Yes," I said. "She screeched and pointed her finger at Mrs Triggs, saying 'she stole it'. Meaning the brooch, of course."

"Now, I want the three of you to listen carefully," said Whittle. "Did you notice Mrs Triggs wearing the brooch *before* Lady Geraldine's outburst?"

"I didn't," I said, "but it was dark, and I had no reason to notice it."

Milo and Pixley murmured their agreement.

"Might Lady Geraldine have been pointing at someone other than Mrs Triggs?" asked Ainsley. "She didn't name Mrs Triggs specifically."

"Well done, Sergeant," said Whittle. "What about it?"

Milo tugged at the bar towel on his shoulder. "Clever idea, but no one else was wearing a brooch."

Pixley licked his lips. "But isn't Ainsley also hinting that Lady Geraldine might have been accusing someone of stealing something other than the brooch? She didn't actually say 'brooch'."

"Intriguing," I said. "But only Milo and Nigel were on either side of Mrs Triggs. If Lady Geraldine had pointed in the wrong direction, it would have pointed to either of them – and since she said 'she', it all seems unlikely."

Ainsley rubbed his forehead. "Did anyone stand near Mrs Triggs from the time of the unloading of the cart to the time Mr Callum Sinclair made the toast?"

I bit my lip, running through the film again in my head. "Everyone did except Pari."

"Pari practically yelled at Beryl from afar," Milo snickered.

"I agree," said Pixley. "Everyone was near Mrs Triggs except Pari."

Ainsley hitched his chair forward. "So what it means is this: anyone might have tampered with the jug except Mr Callum Sinclair, Lady Geraldine, Mr Pixley Hayford, Miss Pari Karan, and Miss Fina Aubrey-Havelock. And everyone interacted with Mrs Triggs except Miss Pari Karan, Lady Geraldine, and Miss Fina Aubrey-Havelock."

"So the only person who could tamper with the glasses was the victim, Beryl Triggs," said Pixley.

Whittle chomped her pencil again. "That gives Mr Sinclair, Miss Karan, Mr Hayford, and Miss Aubrey-Havelock solid alibis. And Lady Craven, of course."

"Which brings us to Miss Dove," said Ainsley, "who very politely confessed to murdering Mrs Triggs last night."

"We'll come to that in a moment," said Whittle. "Now, I want each of you to tell me what you know of the deceased and your relationship to her."

Pixley raised his hand. "My piece is short and sweet. I'd never met anyone in Crickle Hythe – except Ruby, Fina, and the postman – before last night. If you want my initial impression of Mrs Triggs and why anyone would want to murder her, I'll tell you that she was obviously a born organiser but definitely a do-gooder who pushed everyone around. But it still doesn't add up to murder."

"And if anyone was irritated enough to murder Mrs Triggs," I put in, "they certainly wouldn't have planned it. It would have been a murder of passion. Of passionate irritation, that is."

Ainsley smirked. "What about you, Miss Aubrey-Havelock?"

"I'd never met Mrs Triggs before, though I'd been staying with Ruby in her cottage."

"Why are you living with her? I understand you're both students at Oxford."

I flicked away an invisible speck of dust. "We're on temporary leave from Oxford at the moment."

"Oh," said Ainsley. It sounded like the letter *o* was sinking slowly to the bottom of the ocean. "Why?"

"Academics. You know."

Whittle sipped her tea. "We don't. Or more accurately, there's any number of reasons. We are the Oxfordshire Constabulary, after all. Even if we don't have jurisdiction over Oxford itself."

"To be honest, you'll have to ask Miss Datchworth at Quenby College. The principal is away, so she's in charge. She wouldn't tell me why Ruby and I had been given this holiday. Or rather, rustication."

Blessedly, Bertie scampered to the door and began barking. Archie Judson bounced through the front door.

Milo patted a seat next to him. "Over here, Archie."

"Ah, young Judson," said Ainsley affably.

"Have some tea," said Whittle.

Pixley couldn't help himself. "Well, isn't this cosy? Quite a change from London coppers."

Archie chomped a biscuit. "Is it murder after all? Mr Sinclair said it was and everyone at school asked me about it. Thrilling to be part of a murder! What about clues? Can I investigate?"

"Whoa there, son," said Milo. "It's not a game."

Contrite, Archie tilted his head forward. But his swinging legs told another story.

Milo put a hand on Archie's head. "Now, tell the police if you noticed anything unusual last night."

Archie pulled at one of his large ears. "There was one thing."

Milo draped his arm over Archie's chair. "Tell us, son."

"I saw Miss Karan – Etty's mum – searching Mrs Triggs's overcoat."

"How do you know the coat belonged to Mrs Triggs?" asked Ainsley.

"Because it was bright red, wasn't it, Dad?"

"I didn't notice. What was Pari searching for? Did she find it?"

Archie bit into another biscuit. "Well." He drew out the "well", clearly enjoying the attention. "Miss Karan spied me watching her, so she stopped searching Mrs Triggs's coat. She told me she'd been looking for her own overcoat and got mixed up."

"But you didn't believe her," said Whittle.

"Her overcoat was black, so how would anyone mix them up, Mrs Chief Inspector?"

"Properly deduced, young Archie. Well done," she said. Then she gave the slightest nod to Milo.

Taking the hint from Whittle, Milo said, "Why don't you go and do your homework in the snug, Archie?"

Though Archie was small, he lodged Bertie under his arm and retired to the snug. I looked longingly after them, wishing for the simpler days of childhood.

Milo wiped his eye with his forefinger. "I suppose I'm next. Last night I told you everything, but we didn't realise it was murder then."

"Thank you, Mr Judson," said Whittle. "Yes, it would be helpful to hear any of your theories about the murder."

Milo surveyed his hands, as if they held an answer. "It's no secret I found Beryl to be a pill, but I wouldn't kill her. As Mr Hayford said, she was a pain in the proverbial."

"What was your specific flavour of irritation, sir?" asked Ainsley.

Milo leaned back in his chair. "She was always on about

having me host various village events at the Duck. Now, I'm as public-spirited as the next fellow, but I've also got to make a living. Sure, if a group comes in here and orders drinks, it's good for business. But she wanted me to buy the drinks myself."

"I see," said Whittle. "Is that it?"

He folded his hands in his lap. "That's it."

Whittle stirred her cup as if she were conducting a tea ceremony. "You're originally from Ottawa in Canada, I understand."

"Yep. Fought in the big show with the RFC – before it became the RAF, of course. Towards the end of the war, I injured my leg, but it wasn't enough to qualify for the disabled soldiers' pension. But I did receive a one-time gratuity payment. I had a bit saved up, too, so I used the lot to buy this place."

Whittle settled herself back in her chair. "Do any of you believe Mrs Triggs stole Lady Geraldine's brooch?"

"Beryl wasn't a kleptomaniac, if that's what you mean," said Milo.

"Maybe Mrs Triggs had debts and planned to sell the brooch?" asked Pixley.

"But why wear it on your lapel, then? In front of everyone?" I asked.

"Did any of you observe Mrs Triggs going upstairs?" asked Whittle.

"I spotted Mr Triggs and Etty coming downstairs as I was going up," I said. "In their fancy dress, of course. A jester and a fairy."

Since I thought we'd exhausted all the possibilities, I gave my thighs a gentle pat. "Now, if it's not too much trouble, I'd like to see my friend Ruby."

CHAPTER
Thirteen

RUBY BRUSHED each sleeve and pulled down her grey jacket. "Right. I'm through with police officers, regardless of gender. Time to solve this crime."

She marched from the bus stop, her arms swinging with purpose.

Pixley and I scrambled to keep up.

"Ruby is angry," whispered Pixley. "Or maybe 'enraged' is a better word."

Looking at my friend's back and her lack of greeting, I had to agree. I knew she wasn't irritated with us – she was simply so overcome with frustration that she had to push ahead. Proving the police wrong was a passion of Ruby's, not only because she didn't believe in them, but also because she had a well-hidden competitive streak.

We turned up the lane towards Chidden Park. Leaves the colour of red crab apples whirled around in little eddies, guiding us towards the house.

Pixley put a hand on my shoulder. "Wait."

I mirrored his move, putting a hand on Ruby's shoulder.

"Don't look back," said Pixley.

We all stood in a peculiar queue on the stone-flagged path.

"Someone's been following us," he hissed.

"Probably the police," Ruby hissed back.

"I don't think so," he said. "They'd be better at it."

"Who is it?" I asked.

"Search me."

"Let's go," said Ruby, still not moving a muscle. "Then we'll catch them when the moment is right."

She continued her purposeful march up the drive.

Nurse Kattos answered the door, understandably appearing worse for wear. Her eyes were glassy and her usually perfect plait had come undone.

"Lady Geraldine is napping, and I haven't seen Callum. He's probably polishing his guns."

"Is that what he does when he's upset?" asked Pixley.

Her eyes widened. "How did you know?"

"Shot in the dark." Pixley covered his mouth. "Erm, sorry."

We followed Nurse Kattos through one of the saddest sights that can visit a house – the aftermath of a party. There was always something so indefinably pathetic about tidying up the next day, especially for a party that had been such an initial success but ultimately a colossal failure. And no one had lifted a finger to clean the mess. I wondered if the police had ordered it to remain that way.

Reading my thoughts, Nurse Kattos said, "We're having an army of chars up this afternoon to clean. Thank goodness."

"If you don't mind the impertinence," said Ruby, "why are you so short of staff? Lady Geraldine can surely afford to hire more people, can't she?"

She sniffed. "I'm not certain, but since Lord Craven made millions from oil, I expect there's a bushelful of cash in the bank."

"What about Callum? Couldn't he pay?"

"I'm afraid he's inherited his aunt's attitude towards money. Shall we say he's thrifty?"

Then she stopped and twisted her head from side to side, as if Callum or Lady Geraldine might be hiding in a cupboard. "As for why they're short of staff, rumour has it that Lady Geraldine has been a tyrant ever since her husband died."

"How long ago was that?" I asked.

"Twenty years." Her mouth held malicious glee. "Even before she was senile, they had trouble finding staff."

"I can see why," said Ruby. "I remember her calling you stupid."

Nurse Kattos let out a high, braying whinny. "She was on fine form that day. The long and short of it is that no one will stand her insults, so it's down to Callum and me. Fortunately, Callum likes to cook, and we have outsiders come in to clean."

"Why do you put up with her?" asked Pixley.

She stuck her hands in her pockets. "My sister and I came to England for a new life and to make money for our family in Cyprus. When my sister died last year, I became even more determined to stay here."

"As a tribute to your sister?" I asked quietly.

Her chin quivered but her voice was steady. "You could call it that. In any case, my plan had been to take my degree, but Oxford won't accept me. So I'll try another—"

"Try another what?" came Callum's voice.

He ambled into the kitchen, and I noticed a fine line creasing either side of his nose down to his chin. His clothes seemed to hang more loosely on his frame. He had aged overnight.

"Glad you've all been released," he said abruptly. "Aunt Geraldine's puggled, and so am I."

"Puggled?" I asked.

"Sorry. Exhausted. Knackered," offered Callum.

Pixley tapped his foot. "If you don't mind me saying, you're all het up over something. Maybe it's the murder, but I have the distinct impression it's something else."

Callum glanced at Nurse Kattos. For a split second, I thought was more between them than met the eye. From what I gathered, they were both single, and, well, difficult circumstances do have a way of bringing people together ...

Nurse Kattos lit a cigarette. Then she looked at it and quickly stubbed it out. "It's Lady Geraldine."

Why was Nurse Kattos so nervous?

"Is she ill?" asked Ruby.

Callum pushed back his floppy hair. "Not exactly. Perhaps it's another stage of her illness – her brain illness, that is. She's been accusing Atina here of murdering Beryl Triggs."

Atina twisted her apron in her fingers. "I know what you're thinking. It's just the way she goes about insulting me and this is simply the newest addition to her repertoire. But she actually becomes deadly serious about it." She paused. "Pardon the word."

Ruby gave a little cough. "May we see Lady Geraldine about it? We have experience with these matters."

"You won't tell the police?" she asked.

"We have no reason to, but the more clarity we have, the better, in case they ask us directly," said Ruby.

As we ascended the stairs, I asked, "How does Lady Geraldine move up and down the stairs in her wheelchair?"

"We had a lift built," said Callum. "It cost a fortune, but it was worth it because she was absolutely set on keeping her room upstairs."

"Was it working during the gala? I mean, was anyone using it to go upstairs?"

He shook his head, breathing a bit more heavily from the stairs. "We didn't want the children fiddling with it, so we blocked it off. But normally, we'd leave it open. I did use it to help her downstairs to the festivities, though."

Lady Geraldine wore a rich red and orange rug on her legs this morning, and a navy knitted shawl. The vividness of the colours swallowed her pale face.

"These are our neighbours, Lady Geraldine, remember?" Atina said.

She waved away the nurse as if she were a bad smell. "Well?

What is it? I've been watching the robins through the window and I don't like to be interrupted."

"About last night …" Callum cooed.

"Last night? Dear Callum, I can't remember five minutes ago, let alone last night."

"You said you witnessed Nurse Kattos poisoning Mrs Triggs, remember?"

Lady Geraldine's eyes zigzagged to the ceiling. "Now that you say it, yes, the stupid girl did poison that most trying Triggs woman."

Atina bit her lip. She could give as good as she got, after all, so it must have been hard for her to stay quiet.

"Nurse Kattos poured the cider into the glasses. Therefore, she poisoned that ghastly woman."

"How did you know Mrs Triggs was poisoned?" Callum asked.

"It's obvious, isn't it?"

"You don't think she had a heart attack? Or a fit?"

"I've seen a heart attack and it didn't look like that."

Nurse Kattos said, "Lady Geraldine is mistaken, or possibly mistook me for someone else. I didn't help Beryl with the glasses."

Lady Geraldine shrugged. "I told you what I saw." Her eyes narrowed at Callum. "And you should think twice now about having this stupid girl wandering about the house. She'll murder both of us in our beds!"

CHAPTER
Fourteen

MY FOOT SLIPPED on the smear of purple jam streaking the chequerboard floor. Piles of dishes leaned in the kitchen sink, and last night's pleasant smells had vanished, replaced with a prickly tang of rotting milk.

"Mind your step," said Callum. "I expect Nurse Kattos told you an army of chars is coming in this afternoon."

Ruby tiptoed across the floor. "Talking of tidying, may we see the orchard before the rain washes everything away?"

He scratched his head. "I'm afraid not. The police said to leave it alone."

"Ah well, it was worth a try," said Ruby. "By the way, what do you think of your aunt's story about Nurse Kattos?"

Callum's grey eyes softened. "Even if Atina had been pouring the cider, I don't see what it proves."

"You heard about the cyanide found in the glass," said Pixley.

"Aye, and the cyanide in the jug. Just because she poured it from the jug doesn't mean she put cyanide in it. Besides, it would be a wee bit obvious, don't you think? And Atina isn't obvious."

No, she wasn't. Atina Kattos spoke her mind, although a definite watchfulness lurked behind those wide eyes.

"How do you feel about being one of the few people with an alibi?" asked Pixley.

Callum ran his hands through his hair. "I have an alibi? Are the police that certain?"

"We spoke to the chief inspector," I said, "and we confirmed that the only people cleared of tampering with the jugs were you, your aunt, Pixley, Pari, and me. And obviously no one is suspected of putting cyanide in the glasses, except Mrs Triggs herself."

Callum put a hand to his head, as if he'd just remembered something. But I thought he'd been biding his time. "One more thing. I didn't tell the police this, but since you're apparently quite keen on solving this case, then you'll want to know."

"Yes?" Ruby lifted her hand from the door. "Go on. We'll take it with a pinch of salt."

He put his hands on his hips. "If the murder wasn't a random poisoning, the most likely victim wouldn't have been Mrs Triggs. It would have been Nigel, her husband."

Pixley clicked his tongue. "Seems a perfectly harmless chappie to me."

"True," said Callum. "He's a nice enough chiel, but what a gossip. If you want anything to get round the village, simply tell Mr Triggs and he'll spread it faster than mercury on a tile floor."

Ruby twisted her lips, trying to suppress a smile. "Any particular mercury he'd been spilling lately? Perhaps about you?"

Callum blushed, and I felt secretly gratified that someone else suffered from my affliction.

"He'd been hinting to everyone that I was involved with Atina Kattos. And Miss Oliver. Miranda, that is. But it's all simply gossip. He picked on Nurse Kattos since we live in the same house, and Miss Oliver because, well, she turns heads."

Pixley leaned forward. "Look here, old man. If you have been dabbling in a few romantic escapades, no one would blame you. After all, you're a free man, as they say."

Callum looked at him sharply. Then his face relaxed. "Aye, Mr Hayford, that I am."

"Well, thank you for your honesty, Mr Sinclair." Ruby opened the door. "Don't worry, we'll see ourselves out."

Outside Chidden Park's rear door, we traded the smell of rotting milk for rotting leaves, a smell that brought me peace about our inevitable slide into winter. Down the hill, the green grass became a muddy brown around the enclosure.

"Don't look back," hissed Ruby. "Callum is watching us."

"We are rather intriguing," said Pixley. "I'd watch us, too."

"We'll go around the corner and then backtrack through the orchard," she said.

"You can never leave well enough alone, can you?" Pixley said. "A warming hot toddy at the Drowned Duck wouldn't go amiss on a day like this. Perhaps we should let someone else solve this mystery – just for once?"

"Where's your spirit of adventure, Pix?" Ruby asked.

He sighed and I gave him a playful nudge. "I'll buy you as many hot toddies as you want after we solve the case. After all, if we don't solve the case, it's likely I'll end up in the dock."

Following Ruby's lead, we wound through the moss-covered orchard back towards the enclosure. I glanced back at Chidden Park, its windows forming a frowning jack-o'-lantern pattern of disapproval at us. A light glowed in an upstairs window, but I saw no one peering out.

We arrived at the enclosure, where footprints were still scattered about from the night before, hardened into a mass of ridges and troughs.

"What are we looking for?" I asked.

"Let's walk around the perimeter of the fence so we don't disturb anything," said Ruby.

Chidden Park's doves watched us from high above in their wooden dovecote home. They cooed and cocked their heads at us as if we were the ones on display.

"Looks like the police took all the cider jugs," said Pixley.

"They took everything, didn't they?" I said. The trees were bare, save the string we'd wrapped around them; they'd even removed the cider cart.

Ruby rubbed the tree bark and then bent down, sniffing like a bloodhound.

"Erm, Ruby. Anything caught your olfactory attention?" Pixley asked.

"Nothing."

"Then why are you sniffing?" I asked. "I'm the one with the nose, after all, and I don't smell anything unusual."

"Aha!" Ruby scooped up a cigarette butt covered in mud.

"A clue!" Pixley cried.

Wrinkling her nose, Ruby said, "Not a clove cigarette. How disappointing."

"Clove cigarette?" I parroted. What the deuce was she on about? I'd noticed a clove aroma in the air last night, but I'd assumed it might have been mulled wine. Though I hadn't seen anyone drinking it.

Our sniffing expedition was abruptly curtailed by a loud, baritone rumble. "And just what do you think you're doing here?"

Pixley removed his cap. "Ah, Constable. We were poking about to help out with the case, but we promise we didn't disturb anything."

The constable frowned into his moustache.

"I'm afraid my friend likes to joke," said Ruby. "Actually, Mr Callum Sinclair said we could visit the doves here. I'm new to the village and I'm looking for a pet dove, so he said we should take a look at them."

Silent and officious, the constable merely bounced on his feet with his hands behind his back.

"Aren't you going to say something?" I asked. The man was exasperating, really. He could certainly learn how to behave from the chief inspector.

Leaving behind his affable buffoon act, the constable leaned forward, the gold buttons of his uniform straining against his bulk. "If you don't leave right now, I'll report you to Chief Inspector Whittle. I understand you're already in a heap of trouble with her."

"Charlie, look!" came a voice from behind the hedge.

We all ran behind the hedge to find another constable, this one as wiry as a weasel, holding something in his handkerchief.

"It's an empty vial, Charlie," he said triumphantly.

"Good work. Let's get it to Whittle toot suite." He turned on us. "And as for you three, scram!"

"Aye aye, captain." Pixley saluted him and sped off through the trees.

We followed Pixley's lead at a more leisurely pace, but fast enough to signal progress to the constable.

"Well, that was a washout," I sighed.

"On the contrary," said Ruby. "It was most instructive."

"You mean because of that vial the constable found? That presumably holds cyanide residue?"

She shook her head. "Didn't you notice something else?"

I groaned. "You are most trying sometimes, Ruby Dove – you never tell me anything. But I know better than to ask what you mean by that cryptic question."

"But you just have, Feens."

Pixley had stopped on the pathway, waiting for us to catch him up. "So what say you, Ruby? Is the case all wrapped up?"

"No, but I do have an idea about how the murder happened," she said. "Though I haven't the foggiest who did it."

"What do you think about Callum's suggestion?" he asked. "Could it have been a mistake to poison Beryl Triggs rather than Nigel Triggs? It was all so haphazard."

"What if Nigel was actually the murderer, not the victim?" I cried. "After all, Beryl must have been insufferable to live with."

"Nigel Triggs is no prize himself," put in Pixley.

"True. But he probably doesn't think that," I said.

"Clearly, it's time for us to do a little shopping at the village stores, isn't it?" said Ruby.

Just as I took a step forward on the path, a rustling noise rose behind my shoulder. I stopped, listening intently. It didn't sound like an animal. Or at least, it sounded like a large animal.

Ruby and Pixley turned around.

Then a twig snapped. I was quite sure that twig snapping was made by an animal – a human animal, that is.

CHAPTER
Fifteen

"OI, YOU THERE!" cried Pixley, taking off at a run. Though Pixley was a man of substantial stature, he sprinted like a hungry whippet.

A figure dashed through the undergrowth, tripping over a tree stump and falling to the ground. Pixley tramped over a few low bushes and stood within a metre of our fallen friend.

The figure lay still, only the leaves around him trembling.

Pixley removed his cap and scratched his head. Then he leaned in, holding his hand over the face covered by a balaclava, presumably to see if the person were still breathing.

With a sudden jerk, our nemesis popped Pixley in the nose and shot off through the undergrowth.

Yelling with pain, Pixley took a few running steps and stopped.

"Pix!" Ruby and I cried in unison, dashing through the foliage.

"Here, take this to stop the bleeding." Ruby handed him her grandmother's blue handkerchief.

Blood streamed from Pixley's nose, spreading a crimson stain across his lovely white shirt.

"Damn and blast it," came Pixley's muffled voice. "He hit me!"

"Is your nose is broken?" I asked.

"Munno," he said, which presumably meant "dunno".

Pixley removed the handkerchief, allowing us to inspect his small-bridged nose.

"It looks straight," I said, "but let's get you to a doctor."

"The nearest doctor is in Shipton-on-Cherwell," said Ruby. "It's a twenty-minute walk if we hurry."

"Mndphs," said Pixley.

"Do be quiet, Pix," I said gently. "Talking will make the blood flow more."

I turned to Ruby. "How about Miranda at the chemist? Maybe she can help – at least she'll have the proper dressing."

"Splendid idea," said Ruby. "Maybe she can call the doctor if needed."

Pixley gave us a tiny nod.

We set off towards the high street, soon arriving at the village chemist. As we entered, a cheerful bell tinkled against the door.

"And what do you think she said?" Mr Triggs said.

At the sight of us, he abruptly cut off his conversation with Miranda.

"Good heavens!" Miranda rushed from behind the counter. "What happened?"

Her exclamation was justified. If Pixley weren't standing upright, I'd have thought he was a murder victim as well. Despite his best efforts, the blood had trickled down to his trousers, and Ruby's handkerchief had turned from blue to a dull brown.

"Let's go into the back room, shall we?" Miranda guided Pixley through the thick curtains behind the counter.

Mr Triggs brushed the sleeves of his oversized waxed jacket as if droplets of Pixley's blood had leapt onto his coat.

"What happened to your friend?" asked Mr Triggs. "He must be as cack-handed as I am."

"He's not clumsy. He just got into a bit of a scrape," I said.

"Must be a tough chap, then. Well, I suppose if you're a journalist, it's part of the trade, isn't it?"

"How did you know he's a journalist?" asked Ruby.

Nigel tapped his finger against his nose, a gesture I find absolutely infuriating.

Ruby gave Nigel a tight smile. "We never had the chance to express our condolences about the loss of your wife. Please accept our most heartfelt sympathy about Mrs Triggs."

Nigel wiped his eye, but no tears were forthcoming. "It's a tragedy, yes," he said quietly.

"You were fond of your wife, weren't you?" I asked.

Ruby glared at me.

But the inappropriateness of my statement had escaped Nigel Triggs.

"I was so fond of Beryl," he said. "She was the loveliest woman in every way. I keep picturing how we first met: Beryl waltzed into the village stores one morning and, as trite as it sounds, she took my breath away."

"Love at first sight?" Even Ruby couldn't keep a slight note of disbelief out of her voice.

Again, Nigel seemed oblivious to tone. He must've been a good listener if he was the town gossip, but his skill apparently lay in collecting information rather than reading other people. Maybe that's why he didn't mind his wife pushing him and everyone else around.

"Don't get me wrong," he continued. "Beryl had strong opinions about everything and everyone, but she was usually right. I learnt a long time ago to let her call the shots. Sure, my mates teased me about her wearing the trousers in the relationship … but little did they know."

What little his mates did know was better kept that way, I thought.

Continuing my role as the uncouth and blunt friend, I said, "It must've been dreadful to discover she didn't die of natural causes."

I paused. Why not throw in a dash of intrigue? "And about the unfortunate brooch business."

Again, Nigel was unbothered by my insinuations. I wished all murder suspects would be so malleable.

"Beryl was fond of jewellery, and brooches in particular, but she would never ever pilfer anything – no matter how insignificant it might be. And as for this supposed poisoning the police mentioned, I simply don't believe it."

"You mean she had a dicky heart?" I asked.

Ruby glared at me again, but this time the look was mixed with amusement.

"She did at that. The doctor had prescribed some medicine for her erratic heartbeat."

"And she presumably bought the medicine from this shop, correct?" put in Ruby.

"If you think someone tampered with Beryl's medication, it's not true," said Nigel. "Besides, she stopped taking it a few months ago, since the side effects were most unpleasant."

He continued, his voice cracking. "Even if it were murder, I can't imagine anyone who'd harm Beryl. She was such a beautiful person."

If I were to sing Beryl's praises, it certainly wouldn't be about her beautiful character. Efficient, yes. Organised, yes. Perhaps even generous. But beautiful? Ah well, love was truly blind.

Ruby coughed. "We wondered, Mr Triggs, if you …"

She struggled to find the words, so I supplied them for her. "We wondered if anyone had a reason to murder you."

CHAPTER
Sixteen

NIGEL TAPPED his doughy cheek with a nail-bitten finger. "Oh, dear me, no. Of course, we have our usual village tiffs and petty squabbles. They're still squabbles, though. Nothing more than that."

Miranda ushered Pixley back out to the front of the shop. He wore a thick piece of gauze around his face and held a wad of tissues in his hand.

"The patient will recover, I'm glad to report." Miranda piloted him to a chair. "His nose isn't broken, but it was a close-run thing. I suggest he rests somewhere for a moment, at least until the bleeding stops."

"Rest isn't a word in Pixley's vocabulary," said Ruby. "But we'll do our best. Thank you for seeing to him."

"So what did happen?" asked Mr Triggs. "An accident with a door? Or did someone pop him one?"

Before I could utter something gauche, Ruby said, "He's still adjusting to his new narrowboat, which has all sorts of levers and gears. One popped up and hit him in the nose."

She tapped her teeth. "Pix, would you go with Mr Triggs to the village stores to fetch sandwich supplies?"

"What? Why me?" came the muffled reply.

I stepped in. "Women matters, Pix. We need to ask Miranda for help."

At those words, Pixley didn't wait for Mr Triggs to escort him from the shop. Holding his head high as if he were running an egg-and-spoon race, he made a beeline for the door.

Although he looked baffled, Mr Triggs scampered after him. It was unsurprising since he was so used to taking orders from Beryl.

Miranda shuffled papers behind the counter. "What can I get you, Fina? An analgesic for cramps?"

"Actually, we wanted to ask you about Mr and Mrs Triggs."

"I see. You wanted to chat with me in private." She smoothed the papers and sighed. "It's ghastly, especially now the police are convinced poor Beryl was murdered."

"I assume the police have looked at your register," said Ruby.

Miranda stiffened. "Naturally. Routine procedure and all that."

"Has anyone bought cyanide recently?" I asked.

She flipped through the pages of her book, as if she couldn't remember.

"May we have a look?" asked Ruby.

Cheeky. Distinctly cheeky.

Miranda flinched but then slid the book towards us. "Help yourself. I keep all purchases together, but of course customers must sign if they're buying a poison."

Ruby and I leaned over, scanning the register. Clearly, we were thinking the same thing – we were afraid that the smallest movement might make Miranda change her mind about sharing such information.

Pari had bought several boxes of headache tablets, and then a score of names had bought a variety of ointments with unrecognisable scientific titles. Nigel had bought a box of throat lozenges, whilst Callum had bought five. Atina had bought hair treatment, and Beryl had done the same. And then our eyes stopped on the page.

Ruby looked up. "Why did Milo Judson, Atina Kattos, and Nigel Triggs all buy cyanide at the same time?"

Miranda smirked. "The police wondered about that, too. There'd been an outbreak, I suppose you'd call it, of wasp nests in the village. That's why those purchases are all clustered together."

I glanced at Ruby, my suspicions rising about those three people.

"But that's only who bought it," Miranda said, reading my mind. "Since they presumably stored it at home, anyone might have accessed it – if they knew where to look."

Suddenly, Miranda slammed the book shut in our faces. "I don't know why I'm telling you this. It will get me in trouble with the police, and I certainly don't need any more of that."

"We'll keep it under our hat," said Ruby. "But a little speculation won't go amiss, will it?"

Miranda's eyes narrowed. "You two are troublemakers, aren't you?"

I poked my chest. "Us?"

She cackled. "Don't worry, I'm a troublemaker too. Life is too short to play games. Or rather, it's too short to play boring games."

"Why would anyone kill Mrs Triggs?" I asked. "Everyone says she was bossy, but surely that's not enough of a motive."

She twisted a strand of hair around her thumb. "Bossy, pushy, interfering. Yes, all of that."

Ruby raised an eyebrow. "You said 'interfering' – what do you mean?"

"Well, you've seen Mr Triggs. He knows everything about everyone. Naturally, Mrs Triggs would learn some of it, though oddly enough she wasn't a gossip herself. It was the little things she'd interfere with. For example, she'd give Milo unsolicited parenting advice since he's raising Archie on his own."

"What happened to Archie's mother?"

"He doesn't talk about it. None of us know."

"Did she also give such advice to Pari about raising Etty?" I asked.

"Oh, did she ever. But you know Pari. Or maybe you don't."

"Let me guess," I said. "She told Mrs Triggs to go to the devil."

"Bingo." Miranda smiled. "You can't tell Pari to do anything."

"Talking of Pari, how did you two meet?" I asked.

She shrank back a little. "Meet? Oh, it was at a racing event," she said dismissively. "After she divorced her husband." Her jaw was taut, and a hint of defensiveness had crept into her voice.

Sensing the shift in tone, Ruby coughed. "Did Mrs Triggs give anyone else advice?"

"Anyone who would listen, really. Or rather, anyone standing within five feet of her. Beryl tried to tell me how to redesign this chemist shop. Then she told Callum he should fire Nurse Kattos and get in a proper nurse."

"Isn't Atina Kattos a proper nurse?"

"Beryl was a fair lady, but somewhat prejudiced. Because Atina had done her training course in Cyprus, Beryl thought it wasn't up to snuff."

I giggled involuntarily, imagining Mrs Triggs doling out advice to Lady Geraldine. "I assume she steered clear of telling Lady Geraldine what to do."

Miranda cackled again. "She did attempt it. When they first met, Beryl tried to tell Lady Geraldine that she ought to sell Chidden Park and move into a bungalow."

Ruby and I leaned over the counter.

"And Lady Geraldine not only called her a few choice names, but she also hurled a vase at her. It hit Beryl's feet, causing a few scratches. But her aggressiveness worked – I don't remember Beryl ever giving her advice again."

Taking advantage of the lighter mood, I asked, "We wondered if Mr Triggs might have been the intended target, not Mrs Triggs."

"Because he's a gossip?" asked Miranda.

"Well … yes," said Ruby.

Miranda cocked her head. "You think he might have used his gossip to extort someone?"

"It did cross our minds," said Ruby.

Her eyes wandered to the ceiling. "Nigel? Extorting money? No. He's as innocent as a newborn baby. Besides, the village stores is doing a brisk trade, especially since the shop in Shipton-on-Cherwell closed. He and Beryl lived a modest life, although social status was important to Beryl since she married down, as it were."

"What do you mean?" I asked.

"Beryl grew up in a highly respectable upper-middle-class home in Berkshire. Her mother was from Dorset and her father from Toronto. She and Nigel *did* fall in love – and you must've noticed how devoted they were to each other. So she took a step down by marrying him, so to speak. Or maybe two or three steps down. I didn't have the sense she resented it, just that she wanted to compensate for it."

"How did she do that?"

Miranda traced a finger along the embossed cover of the poison book. "At first, she bought expensive tailored clothes. The hats and suits didn't sit right on her, though, and she knew it. So she tried filling her house with beautiful things. This project failed when many people declined her invitations to dinner. Then she took to good works. Good works suited her perfectly, and gave her social standing, even if it was in a tiny place like Crickle Hythe."

"Did she have her sights aimed higher? To become famous in Oxfordshire, for example?" I asked.

"I expect so. Organising fêtes, charity work, you know the sort of thing. Makes my skin crawl, quite honestly, but to each their own, I say."

"Thank you for your honesty," said Ruby, turning towards the door.

Outside the shop, a few flyers on the noticeboard flapped in the breeze. I stared at them, trying to remember why they seemed significant.

I dashed back into the shop and Ruby followed a few steps behind.

"One more thing," I said. "I was curious about local politics – an occupational hazard of being a student of history. I remember reading about a local meeting on canal regulations. Something about a proposed development. Does that mean anything to you?"

Miranda shifted her weight onto one leg. "Sorry, I never pay attention to local politics. There's enough village intrigue to keep anyone satisfied."

CHAPTER
Seventeen

ARMED WITH A SACKFUL of sandwich supplies, we tramped along the canal to Pixley's narrowboat. The sun played peekaboo with us through the clouds, as shy but inquisitive as a feral cat.

Ruby veered away suddenly, avoiding a tree root slithering across the path. She stopped and stared at the root, as if it were channelling her thoughts. "Miranda was lying when you asked her about that local meeting."

"Mmph?" asked Pixley, whose normally clear voice was still hampered by the gauze across his mouth.

So I recounted how I'd found the council meeting notice in Pari's garage, and Miranda's odd insistence that she knew nothing of it.

"But why deny it?" asked Ruby. "Does it have something to do with the canal, or this proposed development?"

"Haven't a clue," I said.

She patted Pixley's hand. "Once you've recovered, would you ring a newspaper chum to ask about any news regarding a development near Crickle Hythe?"

Pixley lifted his chin, agreeing to her request.

"Talking of news," Ruby continued, "did you learn anything

more from Mr Triggs?"

"Mhh … Milo. Debt," he gurgled.

I snapped my fingers. "When we entered the pub, remember how Milo was speaking on the telephone about some scheme?"

"Mmph," Pixley said.

Ruby stopped. "Now you mention it, I remember Milo organising a little game with the children last night. A betting game, involving sweets rather than money."

"Right," I said. "So Milo might be in debt. I still cannot fathom how killing Mrs Triggs would solve that problem."

"Well, it's the first solid motive we've found," said Ruby.

"What about Nurse Kattos? Or Miranda?" I asked. "Do they have motives, such as extreme irritation with Mrs Triggs?"

"Nurse Kattos I can imagine, and maybe even Callum, but why Miranda?"

I told them how I'd overheard Miranda and Milo speaking at the gala.

"Intriguing. What you said confirms that Pari could be jealous of Milo if he's having his wicked way with Miranda."

I kicked a pebble. "Still, none of it involves Mrs Triggs. Or even Mr Triggs."

"We considered Nigel as an extortionist, but what if Beryl was the one doing it?" asked Ruby.

"It's possible, but the only person who gives a fig about social position in this village – other than perhaps Lady Geraldine – was Mrs Triggs herself!"

"Maddening, isn't it?" said Ruby.

Through the trees and around the bend, I anticipated seeing Pixley's cheerful green-and-red narrowboat, like a welcome carriage waiting to whisk us away.

Except that the narrowboat had vanished.

"Pix," I called without looking back, "did you moor your narrowboat somewhere else?"

"Mmmrrph!" came the muffled cry.

There was no need for him to translate the meaning.

Ruby dashed towards the spot where the boat had been moored, letting the paper bag of sandwiches slip through her fingers.

Pixley began an awkward trot as well, holding his nose high.

I held him back. "Wait here. Don't worry – we'll find it."

Leaving Pixley behind, I dashed after Ruby, hopping over tree roots and rocks along the canal path. All I could see ahead were a few willow trees dipping their branches into the rushing water.

"Feens!" called Ruby.

She vanished around the bend.

Something wasn't right. Ruby's voice wasn't excited – it was panicked.

Stumbling on a rock, I soon righted myself and flew over the pathway now covered in soft moss. In the distance, I spotted a hand bobbing in the current. Then a head covered in black hair.

"Ruby!" I screeched, slipping and sliding down the bank.

She must have slipped into the canal, but she had grasped the bending willow tree, which was now keeping her afloat. The canal had swelled with rainwater from the past week, so it had an unusually fast-moving current.

"Here, give me your hand!" I called.

Both of her hands grasped the tree branch, and she wasn't about to let one go.

"Grip higher on the branch."

She did so and, with a jerky movement, grabbed my hand.

I pulled her towards me, but that sent me rolling onto my backside.

Her free hand flailed, and she went under again.

"Fee—" she burbled.

Frantically, I searched the path for something. Anything. Finally, I spotted a broken tree branch.

It was too short. I considered jumping into the canal, but I wasn't strong enough to swim against the current, let alone carry Ruby with me.

The tree branch would have to do.

I flattened myself on the ground and stuck out the branch. It was steady over the water, right above where Ruby's head bobbed.

Every time she came up, she reached out an arm, but it wasn't enough. If I lowered the branch, I'd lose my leverage over the bank. But I had no choice. Letting it droop near the water was just enough to allow Ruby to grasp it.

I desperately held onto the other end of the branch with my chin buried in the cold mud. At least Ruby wasn't actively drowning now, as she had a firm grip on my stick and the willow branch.

"I can't pull you in," I gasped, spitting mud everywhere.

Suddenly, a hand pulled at my back.

I flipped over, letting the branch go.

"No!" I cried.

But Pixley had grabbed the branch holding Ruby just as I'd let go.

My focus had been so complete I hadn't heard him behind me. Thank goodness he had followed us, since he now had a firm hand on the stick.

"That's right, Ruby," he said, as if he were coaxing a creature into the house. "Let go of the willow and put both hands on the branch."

"I can't! I'll drown!"

"Trust me. I won't let you go – I promise."

Grimacing, Ruby let go of the willow and grasped the branch.

"Ow!"

She'd pricked herself, sending drops of blood into the water. With bold hands, she grasped higher on the branch, coming closer and closer. An inch at a time.

Finally, she reached the water's edge, where Pixley and I hauled her onto the bank.

She lay in the mud, blinking at the sky.

Pixley looked at me. "I heard you screaming, so I had to come."

"Glad you did. I couldn't have pulled her out with that branch." I peered at the soaked bandage on his face. "At least you can speak now."

"My nose stopped bleeding for a moment." He raised his head again, but then dropped it momentarily. "I thought Ruby could swim."

Frowning as she lay on her back, Ruby said, "Ruby can swim. If Ruby doesn't twist her ankle as she falls into the water."

I stared at her ankle. "Is it sprained?"

She slowly clicked her toes together. "I think it was momentary."

"You've lost your shoes," I said.

"That's not all we've lost," sniffed Pixley. "Where on earth is my narrowboat?"

"Don't worry, Pix." Ruby flung her arm towards the canal. "Your chariot is downriver, caught in some reeds. It won't be going anywhere in a hurry. I rushed back to tell you that when I slipped into the water."

Pixley let out a great whoosh of relief. "I'll toddle off downriver then."

"Do you mind if I lie here for a moment?" asked Ruby, not moving a muscle.

"Of course not," said Pixley. Then he jerked his head up. "Would you go, Red? My nose is starting to bleed again."

Wiping mud from my chin, I said, "First, I'll find Ruby's shoes. Then we'll take care of the narrowboat."

"I'm sure they're gone forever, Feens."

"Nevertheless."

Trotting back and forth like a terrier sniffing three tracks at once, I went up one pathway and then took another, avoiding slippy paths that might send me tumbling into the water like Ruby.

In the distance, I spotted Pixley's narrowboat firmly tangled in the reeds. I let out a stream of air – although we were all the worse for wear, we were all in one piece. Safe.

As if to encourage me, the sun broke through the clouds, warming my arms still caked with earth. This part of the canal had a dry, rocky pathway, allowing a clear view along the water. A paper bag flailed sadly on a reed in the water, like it was waving goodbye.

With a sharp pang of culinary regret, I realised it resembled our bag of sandwiches. I peered more closely, making out the words "Crickle Hythe" on the paper.

Drat. I was decidedly peckish now that the excitement was over.

Since I hadn't found Ruby's shoes, I retraced my steps to where Pixley and Ruby sat propped against a tree. They'd never looked so vulnerable: Pixley with his ridiculous bandage, and Ruby without her shoes. Her normally shining black hair appeared grey from a distance, but up close I saw it was simply streaks of clay.

A fish splashed in the water, drawing my attention back to the canal.

With a squeal of delight, I pounced on a black court shoe hoisted high on a cattail. I soon found its partner sunning itself on a rock nearby.

With a whoop of joy, I held the swinging shoes high in the air. "Look at what I found!"

Pixley clapped and Ruby smiled.

Then her smile faded.

"Sorry, Feens. Those aren't my shoes."

I fondled the buckle on one shoe.

"They look like your shoes," said Pixley.

"Almost, but not quite." Ruby stared at them. "But I've seen those shoes somewhere before. Where was it?"

"Use your photographic memory, Red," said Pixley.

Squeezing my eyes shut, I played the film of the last day or so in my head. My green Robin Hood shoes. Then my heels. Pixley's pirate boots. Callum's deliberately tattered peasant shoes. Milo's Roman sandals. Pari's glittering butterfly slippers. And Miranda's vampy lattice shoes. Nurse Kattos's serviceable brogues. Who was missing?

My eyelids flickered open.

"Those are Lady Geraldine's shoes!"

CHAPTER
Eighteen

PIXLEY BANGED on the door to Chidden Park.

I pressed the bell.

After a few moments, Pixley thumped his fist against the wood again.

The door finally swung open, revealing a barefoot Callum wearing a loose, unbuttoned shirt. A whisky aroma floated from the doorway.

"What's the matter? What a stushie," he slurred. He wasn't drunk but he had definitely been drinking. Then he looked us all up and down. "And what happened to the three of you? Have you taken to sleeping rough?"

"Where's Lady Geraldine?" asked Ruby, pushing past him into the foyer.

"Upstairs, sleeping."

"And Nurse Kattos?" I asked.

"She went to the shops – in Oxford," said Callum.

"I'll just look in on Lady Geraldine." Ruby began to limp up the stairs.

"We'll all go," I said. Pixley and I each took one of Ruby's arms and we all made our way upstairs.

Callum padded behind us in his bare feet and tapped on the door. "Auntie? Time to wake up."

He pushed the door open slowly, as if expecting someone to be standing behind it. It swung to the side, revealing an empty room. Crumpled linen lay on the bed, and the window was open a crack. Lady Geraldine's wheelchair stood dejected in the corner, with her droopy shawl thrown over the back of it.

The whistling wind drew my attention to the window. I ran across the room and pushed it open. Directly below it sat a flower bed with soft indentations, presumably made from the ladder the skeleton had used the night before. Perhaps the skeleton had returned and carried off Lady Geraldine. Perhaps this really was one of those cases of a madman wandering the countryside. Perhaps—

"What the tarry has happened to Auntie?" Callum paced in his bare feet, staring at the floorboards for answers.

"Where's your ladder?" I asked.

His hair flopped over one eye. "We do have a ladder – somewhere in the garden."

Pointing to the window, I said, "Someone must've propped it against the house and carried away Lady Geraldine."

He ran to the window. "But then where's the ladder? And why would they do such a thing?"

"They must have hidden it," I said.

Ruby put a hand on Callum's arm. "Would you have heard anyone entering or leaving the house?"

"I was in the room farthest from here, so normally I'd say yes, but—"

"If someone were quiet enough …" put in Pixley.

Callum pushed back his hair, revealing the fine worry lines on his forehead. "I'll call the police. She might have wandered off. Senile people do wander, don't they?"

But we all knew Lady Geraldine couldn't wander anywhere without her wheelchair.

"Give me that pie, Red." Pixley licked his lips. "I'll make quick work of it."

"Not on your life." I plunged my fork into the golden crust of my shepherd's pie. Clouds of steam arose from the lovely, gooey mess inside.

Ruby leaned over the table. "Could you two look a little less cheerful? It seems rude to be enjoying yourselves so much."

The Drowned Duck was quiet, and only Milo was about, counting the money at the till. The wind had arisen outside, hurling dead leaves against the window and bursts of cold air from the door.

Pixley made an O with his mouth, chewing a hot piece of his sausage. "No one's here, Ruby, so it's the best time to put on the old nosebag. Don't worry, Red and I will look appropriately sombre as soon as we finish."

"Must keep our strength up," I agreed, taking a gulp of my cider.

"Where is everyone?" asked Ruby. "Whittle told everyone to be here by now."

When Callum had telephoned the police about Lady Geraldine's disappearance, the chief inspector told us to wait at the pub whilst they searched the canal. Callum had said he'd wait for Nurse Kattos to return from her shopping trip to Oxford.

Sergeant Ainsley then telephoned other witnesses to Beryl Triggs's death and instructed them to gather at the pub. I assumed Whittle's sheep-herding tactic for suspects aimed to keep us from spreading rumours far and wide.

Pixley took a swig of his pint. "Mark my words, the old girl is a goner."

Ruby tapped Pixley's hand. "It's no time to joke."

"Why are you so worried about appearances, Ruby?" I asked.

She twisted her earring. "I'm so unsettled by Pixley's

encounter with that person following us. We're clearly being watched."

I set down my glass. "Well, that's what the note from the skeleton said."

"I'm enjoying my meal, and I'm going to continue enjoying it until someone stops me." Pixley waved his fork. "I must say, I'm surprised by you two."

"Surprised at what?" Ruby snatched a slice of bread from Pixley's plate.

"Hey! I thought we were supposed to be in mourning."

"You convinced me otherwise." Ruby munched on the bread. "Now, what's this about a surprise?"

Pixley gave us an exaggerated eye-roll. "Well, why haven't you two asked me about the masked figure that socked me on the nose?"

Ruby and I stared at each other. Then, either because of exhaustion, the food, or the general absurdity of our situation, we burst into a fit of giggles.

Pixley sighed. "I can't take you two anywhere, can I?"

I wiped my damp eyes. "Go on, Pix. Tell us."

"That's just it. I haven't a clue, but there was something deuced familiar about him."

"So at least you know it's a him," said Ruby, never willing to assume that women couldn't be just as strong as a man.

I glanced at the bar and whispered, "Could it have been Milo?"

Pixley smirked. "I'd know if it was Milo. No, it was someone I haven't met particularly recently."

"Well, while you noodle around on that problem, have you found out anything else of interest?" asked Ruby.

"I did, dear heart, after speaking to my chum Freddie at the *Daily Wink*."

"What a hopeless name for a newspaper," I said.

"What did Freddie say?" asked Ruby.

"He found a development scheme that may affect Crickle

Hythe. Pari's garage and Miranda's chemist shop are up for discussion. Or rather, the land is what's under discussion."

"Not the pub or the village shop?"

"Unlikely, though I fancy they'd still be affected. Apparently, it's a very popular plan with local bigwigs and the public," Pixley said.

"Could the scheme benefit Pari or Miranda?" I asked.

He waved his fork. "Freddie says they wouldn't get much from the project if the latest cases are anything to go by."

Milo strode over and planted his hands on the table, subtly filling the space with his muscular frame. "So, the old lady has finally popped her clogs, hasn't she?"

Pixley jabbed his fork in the air. "See? Judson is also taking the flippant approach."

"Gallows humour," said Milo. "Had to pick it up in the war."

"What's your theory, Milo?" I asked.

Widening his stance, he waved his arms in a chopping motion. "It's like this. Beryl dies of a heart attack because she's so shocked at Lady Geraldine's accusation. Now, Lady Geraldine is senile, and senile people wander. The old bird has a lot of strength in her, so she climbs out of the window – or simply walks out of the house and locks up behind her. Then she also dies of a heart attack or something."

Pixley dabbed the corners of his mouth. "Fascinating theory, Judson, most fascinating. The problem is the old cyanide issue for Mrs Triggs, and the fact that Lady Geraldine didn't have a key, so she couldn't have left her room and locked it from the outside. She would have had to climb down a ladder – but no ladder was leaning against the house. Besides, Lady Geraldine has trouble walking, much less climbing a ladder."

The front door slammed and Archie tramped in. An inquisitive Bertie trailed behind him, ears flopping happily.

"Can I do my homework at the bar, Dad?"

"Sure, son. At least for now. Remember to work on your sums so you can help out your dad with finances."

With perfect seriousness, Archie said, "I'm no better at maths than you, Dad."

Milo sighed.

"Talking of maths," said Pixley, "this pub must be a gold mine if you have all the traffic coming to and from Oxford."

Milo's pointy eyebrows rose. "We bring in the punters, but this place positively eats cash." He pointed at the ceiling. "The thatch alone could do me in. But I think the problem might be solved soon."

Before we asked about this presumed miracle, a whoosh of air drew our attention to the entrance again.

Pari lumbered through the door, walking on the outer edges of her feet. Her dangling gold earrings and floaty pink frock made her look like a birthday cake. Etty flounced alongside, her pigtails bouncing jauntily.

"That blasted chief inspector ordered us here, Milo," said Pari, "but no explanation as to why. Have they caught the murderer?"

"No such luck," said Milo. "And now Lady Geraldine is missing."

Pari slammed her bag on the table. "Bloody police."

"Pari, language," said Milo.

She waved a hand, her earrings flopping about. "Etty and Archie have heard it all before."

From the stool next to Archie at the bar, Etty smirked. Archie's cheeks flamed.

"Callum probably did it," said Pari. "Or Nurse Kattos. Damned incomers. Even if Callum doesn't need money since he lives at Chidden Park."

"Chidden Park eats cash, just like the upkeep on this place does." Milo waved his bar towel around the room.

Puzzled, I asked, "How does Callum's money situation give him a motive to murder Beryl Triggs?"

Pari pointed a finger at me. "If Geraldine has popped off, then it's one of those clever double murders – and Callum or Nurse Kattos did it. Or maybe they did it together!"

"You mean Beryl Triggs's murder was random whilst the real goal was to murder Lady Geraldine?" asked Ruby.

Pari pounded her fist on the table. "Absolutely. Then Callum marries Nurse Kattos and inherits everything from his aunt. Hell, the brooch collection alone must be worth a mint."

"But Pari, we're not positive that Geraldine is, well …" said Milo.

"Geraldine is what?" asked Miranda. She drifted in with Nigel in tow.

"We were speculating about what happened to Lady Geraldine," said Pari.

Nigel and Miranda joined our table, ordering tea and a pint.

"The village is positively crawling with police," said Miranda. "And everyone who comes into the chemist's wants to know what's going on."

Taking a sip of his bitter, Nigel wiped his mouth with the back of his hand. "Same in the shop. I've been running about all day, especially because …"

Pixley slapped his knee. "I say, what about a round of darts?" He turned to Milo. "Do you have darts?"

Milo jerked his head back. "In the taproom – near the restroom. No one is back there, so we might as well make use of it."

Ruby and I held back, I expect out of a vague sense of propriety.

"Smashing idea, Pixley," said Pari. "We'll have to wait around for the bloody police, so let's pass the time with a game."

Warming to the challenge, Milo said, "Let's take bets."

Ruby and I smiled at each other.

CHAPTER
Nineteen

THE DARTBOARD HAD BEEN the site of many a battle. To say it was pockmarked was an understatement: the red and green paint had chipped off, and so had many of the numbers. Indeed, the taproom itself had an air of decline, unlike the rest of the pub.

Callum and Nurse Kattos had joined us, though they both begged off from playing the game. Worry – or guilt – creased their faces as they sat quietly in the corner. Callum nursed a whisky whilst Nurse Kattos drank coffee.

Each of us had a turn at the dartboard, but Nigel's hand shook too much, so he soon took a seat next to Nurse Kattos.

I struck a bullseye on my first try.

"Well done, Feens," said Ruby. "I've never seen you play darts before."

"Only a few times," I said as I struck gold again.

Milo stepped forward next, his eyes narrowed on the board. "Fina's clearly a card sharp. You know, like the guy who pretends he's new at a game but then takes all the winnings."

With a little stamp of my foot, I insisted, "I've only played a few times."

"A likely story." Milo winked at me. "Now that we're down to the three of us – Miranda, me, and Fina – it's time to place your bets."

Miranda brushed Milo's arm as she scooped up a dart. In the corner, Pari flinched. Interesting. So that triangle between the three of them wasn't my fanciful imagination.

Miranda's dart sailed near the bullseye, but not quite.

It was my turn.

Cricking my neck and then my hands, I picked up the dart.

"Steady on, Red," Pixley chuckled.

"Go ahead," I said. "Laugh all you want."

I squinted, aimed, and threw the dart. Then I squeezed my eyes shut.

"Well done!" Everyone applauded.

Milo stretched out his hand and I shook it. "A worthy opponent, Fina. But are you ready to see the real professional?"

Suddenly, my stomach churned and then tightened. "Must dash!" I called, scampering out of the room.

Something I'd eaten hadn't agreed with me.

Where on earth was the toilet? The Drowned Duck had so many nooks and crannies. I wound my way around behind the bar, through the snug, and finally found the Ladies.

After finding relief, I combed my fringe in the mirror. It only made it stick up on end. But at least all the mud had been cleaned from my face.

Ready to rejoin the others, despite the lingering revolution in my stomach, I pushed on the door. It didn't open, so I pulled on the handle.

It still didn't open.

Curious. Nothing was wedged into the door jamb, and nothing else obstructed the door.

I rattled the doorknob. Nothing happened.

"Hello?" I called tentatively.

Maybe Bertie had dragged something in front of the door? But he was a tiny creature. I'd seen him carrying around a stuffed toy pheasant earlier, so perhaps he'd wedged it underneath.

"Bertie," I called. "Are you there?"

I'd seen him responding to his name before, so I expected to hear a yap.

But there was only silence.

Right. The only thing to do was to remove the obstruction, so I readied myself to ram the door.

Before my body hit the door, it swung open, sending me onto the floor in a somersault motion.

I was now on my back, staring at the flickering light on the ceiling. Then something covered the light and lifted me from the floor. I opened my mouth to scream but whomever had grabbed me pushed a cloth into my mouth. I shook my head like Bertie destroying his toy pheasant.

The figure swung me over their shoulder, clasped my legs and dashed out of the back door.

Try as I might, my tongue's brave efforts at pushing the cloth from my mouth proved fruitless, so my screams sounded like muffled groans. I couldn't kick my captor, and pounding on their back with my fists achieved nothing.

Though I was nearly upside down on my captor's shoulder, I saw the warmly lit windows of the Duck in the background, and even Ruby and Pixley clinking their glasses together.

In that moment, I'd never felt so alone. Ruby and Pixley had absolutely no idea I'd disappeared, and I'd probably be killed and—

My spiral of apocalyptic self-pity was interrupted by a rude jolt as my captor flung me into the back seat of a motor car. I squirmed and wriggled my mouth from side to side. Finally, the cloth came free and I managed a dry shriek.

I shrieked once more upon seeing my captor's face.

It wasn't a face at all. It was the skeleton.

The skeleton drove around winding lanes, sending me rocking back and forth for an eternity in the back seat. I became queasy. So queasy, in fact, that all I wanted was for the motor car to stop.

My wish was soon granted. The car came to a grinding halt, sending me hurling into the seat.

This is it, Fina. It's the end.

A thrush twittered outside, its cheerful tone mocking my desperate situation. But the rest of the space filled with silence.

I lay flat on the back seat, squirming about. The door opened next to my head, and the skeleton placed a blindfold over my eyes.

I gulped.

The skeleton whispered, "Don't worry. I'm not going to hurt you, I promise."

I had no choice but to allow the skeleton to guide me from the car and onto soft ground.

"That's right," he said. "Just a few steps into the house. Nearly there."

"Ow," I yelped through the cloth. I'd stubbed my toe.

"Apologies. Now, we'll go up these stairs."

Upstairs, he led me into a room, loosened the blindfold, and removed the cloth from my mouth. He ran from the room before I could say anything. When I pulled down the blindfold, I was confronted with a blacked-out room – even the windows were painted black. But a comfortable-looking bed stood in the corner, and a basket of food sat on the table.

Even I didn't want food at that moment. I searched the room for gaps in the floorboards and ran my fingernails along the windowpanes. I assumed it was pointless to scream, as the skeleton had undoubtedly picked a hideaway well away from civilisation.

In the basket was a metal biscuit tin. Though the tin itself was quite light, it could make a handy weapon if I stuffed it with heavy items. The bed posts sported pointed finials, so I twisted them and pulled. Finally, one popped off. I did the same with the other three and placed them in the tin. I swung it a little, rattling the metal inside. Yes, it was perfect.

I considered the door. It swung inward, so that would help with the element of surprise. The skeleton wasn't too tall, though he was definitely taller than me. I'd need some leverage or height if I planned to bring this tin crashing down on his skull.

Shifting the table was pointless as the scraping noise would surely send him running in. There wasn't a chair in the room, either.

I spotted a rug underneath the bed. It would do. I lifted each table leg in turn and slid the rug underneath. Then I slid the table on the rug towards the door.

Perfect. Everything was ready.

The only obvious way to send the skeleton running through the door was to scream.

So I began softly, tentatively, and then gained steam. Soon, I was at full throttle like Enrico Caruso.

Heavy footsteps trudged up the stairs, not the hurried footsteps I'd expected. I heard the resignation in them. Whomever the skeleton was, his heart certainly wasn't in this kidnapping business.

The footsteps stopped and a key scraped in the lock.

I crouched on the table with the tin above my head.

The door opened and I smashed the tin on the skeleton's head, sending him into a crumpled heap on the floor.

I waited a moment to be confident he wasn't shamming, and then leapt off the table. Though my instinct was to run, curiosity overcame me. Who was this skeleton?

He lay face-up on the floor, so I rolled up the knitted balaclava helmet covering his head. When I'd reached the nose, I yelped in surprise.

It was the last person I expected to see in Crickle Hythe.

It was the face of Niall Rafferty.

CHAPTER
Twenty

SITTING ON MY HAUNCHES, I contemplated his peaceful face – the crooked nose, the long jaw, and the mop of dark hair. I'd met Niall on our ill-fated weekend in Cornwall, where he'd become entangled with a murderer. Though the murderer had escaped, or possibly drowned in the sea, Niall was left behind to face the proverbial music.

Press coverage of the murder had devastated his Harley Street psychotherapy practice, and I suspected the police must have been watching him. So it wasn't surprising he was on the run.

But why kidnap me? Surely he didn't need this elaborate charade just to tell me something. And was he the masked man who had punched Pixley in the nose? It would be logical, I supposed. There was something familiar about his gait, now that I thought about it.

In the distance, a motor car's gears shifted – the only sound besides a few noisy magpies.

I waited, straining my ears. The car had accelerated and was definitely coming closer.

Scanning the room and Niall's face one last time, I threw on my jacket and scampered downstairs. The kitchen window overlooked the road, so I squeezed myself between the sink and a worktop to watch for the oncoming motor car.

A black Austin slowed, ambling over potholes in the road. I pressed my cheek against the window, trying to recognise the driver. As the car turned onto the drive, blond hair stood out against the black interior.

It was Sergeant Ainsley. And someone else sat beside him, though I couldn't see their face. Presumably our dear chief inspector.

Ainsley stopped the car and got out, his confident feet crunching up the drive. The other door opened, but the person didn't get out.

With hands on hips, Ainsley looked the house up and down, as if he were prepared to make an offer on it.

"Shall I search the house, ma'am?"

He squinted at the upstairs windows.

I held my breath. The police mustn't find Niall. But my grey cells didn't fancy helping me with this puzzle of what action I should take next.

Another motor car approached on the lane. My limbs quivered, and my mouth tasted foul. It must be another police vehicle.

As the green Swallow Saloon turned up the drive, I almost squealed with delight. It was Ruby and Pixley!

I searched for something to throw from the window to draw their attention. But I stopped abruptly, realising it would only bring the police running inside.

Footsteps coming alongside the house jerked me back into action. I lowered myself onto the floor, pressing my back into the soft, mildewing wall.

The footsteps stopped right outside the window. I held my breath, hoping my hair colour blended into the wooden work surface.

"Hi!" called Pixley.

For a moment, I thought Pixley was speaking to me.

Then he continued, "Nothing here – just an abandoned house. Can't see anything moving about inside."

From the other side of the house, Ainsley called, "Nothing here, either."

A pain suddenly shot up my leg. A blasted leg cramp. But I suppressed my yelp, not daring to make a sound until the motor cars started.

Just as the shooting pain became unbearable, one of the cars revved its engine and sped down the drive.

Wincing, I slid myself up against the slimy wall until I was level with the window.

Then a finger tapped on the glass, sending my heart hammering.

Thank goodness. It was Pixley.

At the same moment, Ruby rushed through the door and into the kitchen, grabbing me by both arms. "Are you all right? Are you hurt?"

"Only a little shaken," I croaked. "Let's get out of here before the police return. I'll explain everything on the way."

———

"Well, I'm damned," breathed Pixley. "So you coshed the poor bugger." He turned the driving wheel to the left, onto the narrow dirt lane.

"So you're telling us that Niall is lying upstairs, completely unconscious?" asked Ruby. "Should we just leave him, Feens?"

"What else can we do?" I said with a stab of guilt. "If we wait for him to wake, the police might wonder where you are and start searching. If we call a doctor, the doctor will alert the police. And besides, I didn't hit him that hard."

"Hell hath no fury," said Pixley.

"I'm not a woman scorned, Pixley Hayford," I said. "Niall must have had an excellent reason to kidnap me."

"Well, we can't worry about him too much at the moment," said Ruby.

Pixley clicked his tongue. "We didn't tell you, Red. They found Lady Geraldine."

"Do you mean they found her body?" I asked.

Ruby and Pixley nodded.

"The police found her floating in the canal — at about the spot you found her shoes, Feens," said Ruby.

"She was exasperating, but I admired her feisty spirit," I said. "And no one deserves to die in such a way."

We sat in silence for a moment, listening to the gentle whir of the engine.

Ruby turned to me from the front seat. "Before we speak to the police again, I have a question for you."

"Go on," I said.

"Close your eyes," she said.

Pixley snickered. "The great and marvellous Madame Dove will tell your fortune."

"Shh, Pix." She gently slapped his hand.

"Right. My eyes are closed," I said. "What now?"

"We'll tap into your splendid memory. As uncomfortable as it might be, cast your mind back to when you were kidnapped from the Duck, taken to the house, left upstairs, and devised your ingenious plan to cosh poor Niall."

"I didn't mean to," I protested. "If I had known …"

"Yes, if you'd known it was your boyfriend …" said Pixley.

"Pix! I'm trying to help Feens concentrate," Ruby said, gritting her teeth.

Continuing in a soothing voice, she said, "Do you have the sequence in your mind's eye?"

"Mmm …"

"Good. What details do you recall?"

Colours flashed in my mind. Movements. A hand. Yes, a hand. What was it doing? It was stuffing something into my pocket.

I slipped my hand into my jacket pocket and pulled out a folded paper and unfolded it on my knee.

"What is it?" asked Pixley.

"It's a news clipping from *The Times*," I said. "One side has the story about Niall. That must be a message to me from Niall – perhaps a clue that he was my kidnapper."

"Let's see." Ruby flipped over the clipping. "On the back, there's a story about a new police recruitment programme in Yorkshire, and another about a cow rampaging through a Welsh village. And another about keeping wooden stairs in peak condition."

"The police recruitment story is intriguing," said Pixley. "I cannot see how the cow or stairs are relevant, though."

I stared at the paper. "Why didn't Niall just speak to me like a normal person? Why kidnap me? And why not kidnap Ruby since she's the real detective?"

"Well, I'm not sure about that," said Ruby, "but perhaps he was worried about you. Your safety."

Pixley shifted gears. "Or maybe …" He gazed at me through the mirror. "Or maybe he simply had to see you."

I snorted. "Just my luck to find someone who has to kidnap me to arrange a date."

"Well, I'm not one to talk," said Ruby, with a rare flash of insight into her own taste in men. "Ian Clavering is a cad."

"Oh ho!" said Pixley. "Codswallop. He's a busy international spy."

We turned down the lane into Crickle Hythe, and the Drowned Duck soon came into view. It was late afternoon now, though the leaden clouds made it look like an evening sky.

"Stairs …" Ruby tapped her teeth. "Niall's clipping reminds me of something. Feens, who might have stolen the brooch when you were upstairs at the gala?"

"The brooch must have been pinched before I went upstairs," I said.

"Precisely. And you didn't notice anyone else go into the room, did you?"

"No. I saw Nigel and Etty coming downstairs as I was going up."

"What if Nigel stole the brooch?" asked Pixley.

"Why?" I asked.

"He might have given it to Beryl," said Pixley.

"Seems too obvious to me," I said.

"Moves Nigel to my number-one-suspect position," said Pixley.

"It does confirm how Beryl was killed," said Ruby.

"You mean *who* killed her, not *how* Beryl was killed?" I asked.

"No, I mean *how* Beryl Triggs was murdered. That's clear now, though I'm still foggy on motive."

Pixley rubbed his forehead. "You know how it is, Red. Once Ruby discovers a key aspect of the mystery, she keeps it under her hat."

Just as Pixley reversed into a parking space near the Duck, Nurse Kattos suddenly sprang from the bushes. She waved her arms at us to stop.

Pixley slammed on the brakes. "What the devil?"

Ruby rolled down her window. "Whatever is the matter, Atina?"

Breathless, she said, "I must speak to you before you see the police."

"Hop in," said Pixley. "Hurry! If I'm not mistaken, I spy a constable's helmet bobbing along the hedge."

Atina flung open my door and hurled herself on top of me.

Pixley continued in reverse, speeding backwards down the lane.

"Stop, Pix, stop!" I cried.

Atina's legs were dangling from the car. She hadn't time to close the door and she was hanging onto the back of Ruby's seat.

Pixley looked over his shoulder. "Crikey. Hang on!" he said, picking up speed.

"Stop! You'll kill her!" cried Ruby.

With a screech of brakes and the smell of rubber, the car rolled to a halt.

"Damn and blast it, Pixley Hayford." I pushed myself up from the seat. "This isn't an American gangster film."

He rubbed his hands together with glee. "Sorry. Couldn't help myself. Is everyone all right?"

"Barely," grumbled Atina.

"I agree," I said. "Next time, Ruby drives."

"And bah humbug to you, too," said Pixley, grinning.

A lady carrying a basket laden with packages passed us along the lane. She held her head straight ahead, but her weasel-like eyes darted towards us.

Righting herself on the seat, Atina asked, "Can we go somewhere where we won't be noticed?"

"Not if you all continue to criticise my driving," said Pixley, even though he shifted into gear.

Ruby tapped her watch. "We cannot go too far, because Chief Inspector Whittle will wonder what's keeping us."

"This won't take long." Atina stared at her fraying sleeves. "First, I must explain about Callum." Her eye twitched. Clearly, her nerves were as frayed as her sleeves.

Ruby turned around. "Are you involved with Callum? Seeing him, I mean?"

She twisted her apron. "Sometimes it's hard to tell."

Ruby and I both rolled our eyes. I said, "Join the crowd."

She stared at us blankly, so I said, "Go on, tell us why."

"Callum runs hot and cold, as they say. But whenever we get close, he reminds me he's still married to that harpy who left him."

Pixley wiped his spectacles. "This will sound gauche, but did Callum ever contemplate giving his wife a large sum of money?"

I blurted, "You mean, to buy her off?"

Pixley grimaced. "More or less, yes."

If Atina was affronted by our question, she didn't show it. "Callum said he tried many times, but she refused."

Ruby leaned forward. "To be clear, Callum inherits Lady Geraldine's estate, correct?"

Atina pursed her lips. "A solicitor confirmed it for us."

"When did you consult a solicitor?" asked Ruby. I could hear a note of scepticism creeping into her voice.

Squinting out the window, Atina said, "Probably a year ago."

Ruby said, "Why are you telling us all of this?"

"I heard you're a detective trio. And that you're the head of it, Ruby."

"That's a bit of an exaggeration," said Ruby. "And besides, if what you say is true, I don't see a strong enough motive for either of you to kill Lady Geraldine, let alone Beryl Triggs."

"Agreed," said Pixley. "Now, what was the real reason you wanted to speak to us?"

Atina's eyes sharpened. "I know who killed Mrs Triggs and Lady Geraldine."

CHAPTER
Twenty-One

ONCE AGAIN, Pixley slammed on the brakes. The motor car was climbing a hill this time, so we began to roll backwards. My stomach lurched and I grabbed the door handle.

"Pix!"

"I'm working on it." A horrible grinding noise came from the front. But we finally crested the hill, where Pixley piloted the car onto a grassy verge.

He turned around. "So? Who did it?"

"And why not tell us straight away?" I asked with a shade of annoyance.

Atina jiggled the door handle absently. "I had to tell you about Callum first because you'd suspect us of murdering Mrs Triggs. And second, I'm the most obvious suspect given Lady Geraldine's accusation against me."

"You mean when Lady Geraldine said you poured the cider into the glasses," said Ruby. "Did she tell anyone besides us and Callum?"

"No, she didn't," said Atina. "That's why I needed to talk to you alone, especially because you might mention it during police questioning."

"Tell us why we shouldn't," said Ruby.

"Because I saw Miranda fiddling with a cider jug."

"What do you mean by 'fiddling'?" asked Pixley.

"Miranda popped the cork. Then she moved in front of the jug, so I couldn't observe her directly. Then she replaced the cork."

"I see," said Ruby. "Under normal circumstances, it wouldn't be noteworthy, but given what happened …"

"But what motive would Miranda have to kill either Mrs Triggs or Lady Geraldine?" I asked.

"I suspect Mrs Triggs had seen Callum and Miranda together," said Atina.

Pixley coughed, obviously trying to be delicate. "And, were they, well, stepping out together?"

Whenever Pixley tried to be diplomatic, his speech harkened to the Victorian era.

"No." Atina rubbed her thumbs and forefingers together. "I don't know. I don't think Callum and Miranda were involved with each other. But in any case, Mrs Triggs probably noticed them and then threatened to tell Pari. If you haven't noticed, Pari is very jealous of anyone close to Miranda."

"So Miranda killed Mrs Triggs to stop her from spilling the beans to Pari," said Pixley. "And presumably Lady Geraldine saw Miranda and Callum together, so she had to be stopped, too."

Ruby smoothed her hair. "It would all make sense except that Miranda is, well—"

"She's a vamp," said Pixley. "A seductive siren."

"You'll have to excuse Pixley," I said. "He has trouble with words sometimes."

"I don't understand," said Atina. "She's seductive – a temptress of sorts – but how does that make her less likely to kill?"

"If Miranda regularly attracts romantic attention, and Pari becomes jealous, then it's not that unusual. Given that, it's not a strong enough motive to kill two people," said Ruby.

Suddenly, we all jumped. Someone had tapped on my window, but I couldn't seem to make my neck turn towards it.

The tapping persisted.

Pixley said, "Are you going to open the window, Red?"

Reluctantly, I turned towards the white face pressed against the glass. Sergeant Ainsley's blue eyes stared back at me.

"Crumbs," I mumbled, rolling down the window. "Hullo, Sergeant. Fancy meeting you here."

"Where have you been? What happened to you?" he asked.

Not unreasonable questions. As I was pondering an answer, Ruby came to the rescue. "We found Fina by the side of the road. She has these attacks sometimes."

"Like poor Lady Geraldine." Pixley bowed his head.

Despite my urge to protest, I kept my mouth clamped shut.

Ainsley's eyebrows raised in clear disbelief. "This is no time for games. The chief inspector has been waiting for you at the pub."

"Ah, we were heading that way, but needed to stop off at Ruby's cottage on the way," said Pixley.

"Then why is your motor car headed in the opposite direction?" asked Ainsley.

"Pixley was just about to turn us around," said Ruby.

"This is a murder inquiry, Miss Dove," he said. "You can attend to household chores at your cottage later."

"It's a women's issue," I said for the second time that day. After all, it had worked before.

And it worked again. Ainsley gulped and turned his head away. But that didn't stop him from rattling on. "Have any of you seen Nurse Kattos?"

My mouth hung open and then shut abruptly as I looked at the seat next to me. Atina must have spied Ainsley walking towards us and had hidden under a pile of coats and blankets draped across the seat.

"We haven't seen her," said Ruby. "Sorry. Is she helping you with your inquiries?"

He smirked. "We have a warrant for her arrest."

Pixley started the car and revved the engine. "Oh dear, well, best of luck and all that. I'll turn this beast around and we'll meet you down the hill at the Duck. Toodle pip!"

The engine roared in reverse and I began to roll up the window.

"Wait." Ainsley stuck his hand through the window, as if he could stop the backwards motion of the car.

"Must dash," said Pixley. "Don't want to disappoint the chief inspector, do we?"

The car continued to move backwards.

"I said wait!"

Pixley ground the gears and the car halted.

"Mr Hayford, please turn off the car. I'm going to conduct a search," said Ainsley.

Before Pixley could switch off the engine, the lump next to me shot out the door.

"Stop! Police!"

Atina sprinted across the heath, heading for a copse of trees on the outskirts of the village. Her speed and agility suggested a champion runner, but Sergeant Ainsley had the advantage of longer legs.

She reached the trees and vanished over a mossy mound down the hill. Ainsley slid on a stone and fell to the ground.

I had no idea if Atina was the murderer, but a little thrill prickled my neck at seeing her escape.

"Let's go to the pub before Ainsley returns with or without Atina," said Ruby.

"Shouldn't we wait?" I asked.

"I'd rather answer any of Whittle's questions before Ainsley returns. He's sure to be hopping mad," said Ruby.

"Sherlock Dove is right," said Pixley as the car ambled down the hill. "I've learnt that from covering many scandals in my day. It's better to control the story before it controls you."

CHAPTER
Twenty-Two

THE CHIEF INSPECTOR and gala guests sat in the snug instead of the bar. What ought to have been a cosy scene was overshadowed by two brutal murders clouding the atmosphere. The air tasted stale and the darts sticking out of the dartboard were mere reminders of a lighter time.

Milo offered me a whisky, which I downed in preparation for my next verbal boxing match with the chief inspector.

Whittle stood by the only window in the room, tapping her fingers on the sill. A sheen of sweat covered her forehead and her lips looked dried and cracked. Her genial personality was clearly fraying at the edges, much like everyone else in the room.

"Take a seat, please," Whittle said in a lower, formal voice. The voice she must've used to interrogate suspects at headquarters.

I squeezed onto the bench next to Pari, who was casually sipping an orange juice. Three empty glasses with orange pulp coating the sides sat on the table.

"What have we missed?" I whispered to Pari.

Whittle heard me. "You've missed a great deal, Miss Aubrey-Havelock. Preliminary findings suggest Lady Geraldine was hit on the back of the head and dumped in the canal. Though we know little at this stage, we do know it was murder."

Miranda twisted her wine glass. "It's not as if any of us wished Lady Geraldine any harm. It was probably marauding students high on cocaine."

Whittle brushed a strand of hair from her eye. "I'm afraid it was someone acquainted with Lady Geraldine. Quite well, in fact: Atina Kattos."

Milo pressed his hands against the bench, as if to leave. "If you know it's her, why are we here?"

"Although we have a warrant for her arrest, I want to make this case airtight. For that, I need your help."

Like a lighthouse in the fog, Whittle's gaze turned slowly towards Callum Sinclair.

Callum stared at his hands. In fact, he hadn't looked up for a moment, even when the three of us had entered. He suddenly banged the table with his fist. "To hell with you. I'm not going to frame Atina for the likes of you."

He rose and grabbed his jacket.

Whittle merely wagged a finger at him gently. It was much more menacing than any verbal command.

Callum sunk back into his seat, returning to his hand-staring occupation.

Ruby coughed. "Might you enlighten us about your theory, Chief Inspector?"

Whittle licked her lips. "It's not a theory. It's fact." Then, as if regaining control of herself, she took a deep breath. "First, we heard that Lady Geraldine believed she saw Nurse Kattos pouring cyanide into one of the jugs. This gave her ample reason to silence Lady Geraldine as a potential witness. Second, Nurse Kattos is in love with Callum Sinclair. Why else would she stand such abuse from Lady Geraldine? She wanted Callum to inherit the estate, so she killed Lady Geraldine so Mr Sinclair inherits the money. Then she marries Mr Sinclair. End of story."

Callum leapt up, the vein across his forehead pulsing purple. "It's a lie. It's a damn lie. Atina would never harm anyone, let alone Aunt Geraldine." Then he snorted. "As to money, I have plenty, so killing my aunt to inherit more would be pointless."

"So you don't deny having a relationship with Atina Kattos, Mr Sinclair?"

He ran his hands through his hair. "It's true enough. But murdering my aunt would have no effect on a basic problem: I have a wife who won't divorce me, and all the money in the world won't change that."

Though I had to agree with Callum, something nagged at the back of my mind. Hadn't Lady Geraldine told me that it was possible that Callum's wife had died recently? Perhaps it was her imagination.

Ruby had overheard my conversation with Lady Geraldine, so I studied her face. She gave no indication anything was wrong, so I decided not to share this titbit. After all, it was most likely Lady Geraldine's fancy.

Pixley cocked his head. "Chief Inspector, are you saying the first murder was random? That Mrs Triggs simply happened to be unlucky enough to drink the cyanide-laced cider?"

Nigel let out something between a gasp and a sob. Mercilessly, Whittle said, "Each of you will now make a statement about whether you saw what Lady Geraldine said she witnessed – Nurse Kattos tampering with the cider."

Ruby coughed. "May I make a suggestion?"

"I have a feeling you will no matter what I say."

Ignoring Whittle's jibe, Ruby continued. "I suggest we refresh everyone's memories by returning to the enclosure."

The temperature in the taproom plunged. Milo, in particular, glowered at Ruby.

Whittle twisted her lips. "Reconstruction isn't a bad idea, Miss Dove. Especially as my sergeant is apparently occupied with chasing after Atina Kattos."

―――

With our heads bent like pilgrims to a holy site, we trudged towards the enclosure. Twilight blanketed Chidden Park, casting a warm glow over the Cotswold stone of the house and amplifying the blue tinge of the grey sky. A bevy of doves greeted us, swooping down before settling on the dovecote nearby.

In a rare show of animal affinity, Ruby made cooing and clicking noises to the doves above her.

"Well, Miss Dove? When you're finished amusing yourself with your namesakes, would you care to enlighten us?" asked Whittle.

"Apologies, Chief Inspector. But these birds hold the key to solving this crime."

We all stared at her.

Ruby cooed again at the doves and then scanned the crowd. "Callum, have you lost any doves lately? I mean, have any died?"

"Ah, no, I don't think so," he said. "One died last year, and it was quite noticeable far away in the field. The white stood out against the brown of the earth."

"Could a fox have taken one?"

Callum approached the dovecote and counted under his breath. "Now that you mention it, one *is* missing."

He turned around and pointed. "Aye, there she is. Now all ten are accounted for, though I cannot see why it matters."

"Thank you, Callum." Ruby smiled again at the doves. "Let's remember that night: we poured the cider over the bread on the trees and the roots of the trees. Then the rifles were fired and we all toasted with cider poured from these jugs."

"Right," said Whittle. "Nurse Kattos tampered with the jug of cider and then Mrs Triggs poured it into the glasses."

"But how could Atina measure just enough for one glass?" asked Pixley. "And be certain that Mrs Triggs would use that specific jug rather than the others?"

"Pixley's right," said Ruby. "It's too risky. And Atina might have even poisoned herself accidentally."

"Not if she were watching closely," said Nigel.

"Atina also had to give Lady Geraldine her injection," I said, "so how could she keep watch on the glasses at the same time?"

"Quite right, Feens," said Ruby. "But what's more significant is that Callum's doves are all alive."

"Bloody hell," breathed Pari. "What's she on about?"

Ignoring Pari's outburst, Ruby continued. "If cyanide were in any of the jugs, it was poured onto the bread on the trees and—"

"The bread!" I cried. "The doves would have eaten the bread soaked in cyanide. At least one of them should have died."

"Precisely," said Ruby. "It's simply not possible otherwise. The three of us inspected the trees this morning and found all the bread had been eaten. The doves couldn't possibly resist the bread."

Pixley squinted at the sky. "Which means the cyanide was *not* in the jug. It must have been put there *after* all the jugs had been emptied."

Ruby nodded. "To make it appear as if a jug were the source of the cyanide."

Whittle uncrossed her arms. "Rubbish. That means Mrs Triggs must have put the cyanide in the glass, which is a ludicrous suggestion."

"Unless she committed suicide," I said, not believing my own words as I said them.

Miranda threw up her arms. "Then it's an impossible murder."

Ruby twisted the toe of her shoe into the muddy earth. "Not quite. The cyanide-in-the-glass theory doesn't work because cyanide poisoning is not exactly instantaneous."

Pixley snapped his fingers. "So Mrs Triggs must have taken the cyanide in another way."

Gesturing to the group, I asked, "I didn't observe her eating or drinking anything else. Did any of you?"

Nigel raised his hand. "I naturally watched my beloved, but I didn't notice her drinking or eating anything."

"Aha," said Ruby. "Thank you, Nigel. Now we can discuss how the brooch fits in."

CHAPTER
Twenty-Three

WHITTLE'S EYEBROWS ROSE. "The brooch, Miss Dove?"

"Yes. I'll come to it," said Ruby. "But first, did the autopsy reveal any marks on the body?"

Whittle shook her head. "It's been less than 24 hours, so all we know is that cyanide poisoning was the likely cause of death. What did you have in mind?"

"Perhaps a pinprick somewhere on the body."

"It's possible. A body usually has little marks, like paper cuts and minor bruises. We usually discount them unless there's a particular reason to pay attention to them."

"If you ask the pathologist to look, I fancy there's a pinprick marking, easily explained by sewing the costumes for the fancy dress event, of course," said Ruby. "When I pricked myself on a branch during a daring rescue by my good friends here, that's when I had the idea."

Pixley gave out a low whistle. "So you're saying the metal pin on the brooch was coated in cyanide?"

"Why not put it in the glasses, as planned? Or the jug?" asked Milo.

"Simply too risky," said Ruby. "Too many people were milling about to guarantee the murderer wouldn't have been noticed.

Also, injected poison would take effect more quickly than if it were ingested by drinking it from the cider, which would also explain how quickly she died."

Whittle rubbed her finger against her lips, as if the reality of Ruby's suggestion was finally settling in. "If Mrs Triggs was killed by a pinprick, it means she was deliberately targeted – not an accidental victim."

"Could she have been jabbed by a sewing needle?" asked Miranda. "Since she was helping with the fancy dress?"

"I considered that, as well as the other obvious needle lying around – Nurse Kattos's syringe," said Ruby.

"But you dismissed it," said Milo. "Because?"

"The sewing needle seemed implausible because it would require someone to prick her in the middle of this event. And in the case of the syringe, someone would have noticed her being injected."

"I'll say," said Pixley. "And what's more, if someone came at me in the dark with a syringe, I'd scream."

"That's right. So it had to be something that wouldn't provoke Mrs Triggs into screaming or yelling. For example, you couldn't simply walk up to her and jab her with a needle because she'd cry out. It needed to be subtler, and a pinprick rarely causes people to yell."

Callum leapt from a bench. "I cannot stand it any longer. Please, just tell us."

"It was the brooch," said Ruby. "She was pricked with Lady Geraldine's brooch smeared with cyanide."

Something rustled behind us.

"Atina!" cried Callum, rushing towards Nurse Kattos. The handcuffs impeded her natural gait, creating a smaller, hunched-over figure. Her eyes darted towards Callum and then looked away.

Ainsley was triumphant. "Finally caught her, ma'am. She didn't come easy, though."

Disgust burned in my throat, a rising sense of outrage at how he described her like a trapped rat.

Ainsley touched her shoulder but Atina wrenched herself away.

Callum's lip quivered. "Would you take off the handcuffs for a moment?"

"Sorry, sir. She might run for it again."

"Oh, go on, Sergeant." Whittle had returned to her indulgent-aunt tone.

Grimacing, Ainsley unlocked the handcuffs and Atina rushed towards Callum.

"All right, that's enough of that," said Whittle. "Now, Miss Dove. Please expand on your theory."

Ruby pushed back her hat. "Not much more to it. The murderer steals the brooch, doctors it with cyanide – wearing gloves or using a handkerchief – and then approaches Mrs Triggs to give her the brooch, accidentally pricking her with it."

"What about the cyanide in the glass and jug?" asked Pari.

"The murderer put cyanide in the jug sometime after Mrs Triggs had prepared the glasses. Then, in the pandemonium after Mrs Triggs collapsed, it was easy to drop cyanide into one of the glasses on the ground."

"So the murderer was the same person who stole the brooch," I said.

"Precisely."

"But that might have been anyone," I said, although I suspected Nigel since I'd seen him coming down the stairs.

"The same is true for Lady Geraldine's death," said Ruby. "Isn't that true, Chief Inspector?"

Whittle licked her lips. "Anyone could have waited until the house was empty, and then went up to Lady Geraldine's room."

"I was still at home, though," said Callum. "And I didn't hear anything."

"You were in another wing of the house," said Pixley. "So the murderer knew you couldn't hear, or they didn't know you were at home."

"Wouldn't it take great strength to carry her?" asked Miranda.

"Lady Geraldine was tiny," said Whittle. "So any of you might have carried her."

"They also might have used the lift," I said. "To move her downstairs."

Callum threw up his hands and resumed pacing. "All of this is very airy-fairy. It still adds up to the same point: any one of us could have done it."

Atina gave him a wistful smile.

"Perhaps," said Ruby. "And Callum and Atina aren't the only ones with reasons to kill. Nigel Triggs might have had enough of his wife, despite an admirable performance to the contrary."

Nigel's mouth opened wide in innocent disbelief.

But Ruby had no time for reactions. She sped onwards. "And talking of relationships, Miranda and Milo might or might not have been having an affair."

"I saw them after the murder," I said, "and they looked very close."

Miranda and Milo studiously avoided each other's eyes.

"What does that have to do with murdering Mrs Triggs?" asked Sergeant Ainsley.

"Mrs Triggs might have discovered the relationship – or heard gossip about it. Then she could have threatened to expose the affair. Maybe Miranda was worried about her reputation."

A few puzzled faces stared back, since Ruby was obviously trying to avoid saying anything outright about Pari and Miranda's relationship.

Ruby continued, "Pari might have been worried about Miranda, and decided to silence Mrs Triggs."

"And me?" asked Milo. "How would this give me a motive to kill Mrs Triggs?"

Ruby whirled round. "It doesn't, but you might have another motive."

He crossed his arms. "Oh yeah?"

"Milo Judson is a risk-taker." Ruby gestured to Milo, as if he were a trained ferret about to perform a trick. "He's also a gambler forever in search of cash."

Milo held up a hand. "Hey, wait a minute. I am in search of cash, but that's for the pub. Purely business. And my little investment flutter should pay off any day now."

I regarded Milo's muscular, confident figure, so self-assured. So sure that his gamble would pay off and that all his troubles would be swept away. I'd seen that look before once in my father's eye, just before my mother stopped him from gambling away our life savings. But Milo didn't have anyone like my mother to prevent him from taking the plunge.

Ruby held up a calming hand. "I do genuinely hope you're correct about your gamble. But it doesn't erase your other risk-taking that's relevant to this case. You claim you're Canadian. Many Canadians joined the Royal Flying Corps – as it was called during the Great War. But an American cousin of mine once shared a little-known fact with me: some Americans posed as Canadians in order to fly in the RFC."

"An admirable lie, I suppose," said Whittle.

"The problems for Milo came after the war," continued Ruby. "If Milo had false identification papers, and had collected a war-related disability gratuity under that false identity, then he could be in trouble. And that's only the beginning."

"Prove it," said Milo.

"Oh, that shouldn't be too difficult once we get started, sir," said Whittle. "But if you tell us the truth, we might find a solution for you."

Milo sat abruptly, as if someone had pushed him onto the bench. "How did you find out?"

Softly, Ruby said, "You used the American word 'restroom' instead of the Canadian 'washroom' or even British 'toilet'. The slip wasn't definitive, but it put the idea in my head. Then, when I discovered Beryl's father was Canadian, I fancied she might have guessed you weren't Canadian, too."

He pulled his hand over his face. "It's true. Archie's mother became pregnant just as the war ended, so I had to stay put. And when Archie's mother died, I had to take care of him on my own. By that time, I'd bought the pub, and I had a few debts. I'd already arranged the fake papers, so it was easier to keep up the lie. More for Archie's sake than anything else."

"Did Mrs Triggs know and threaten to expose you?" asked Ruby.

He rubbed his brow. "Beryl didn't threaten me, exactly, but she kept dropping these little hints. She positively swelled with the power it gave her. She loved having power over others, but I swear I didn't kill her."

"Power," said Ruby. "Yes, that's why so many of you had motives to kill Beryl Triggs. She had power over you."

CHAPTER
Twenty-Four

RUBY'S WORDS had struck home. Everyone was shifting about, staring at their feet – staring anywhere but at her accusing face.

Leaning against a fence post for support, Ruby continued. "When the case began, everyone agreed that Beryl Triggs was bossy and pushy."

"I resent that!" cried Nigel. "She was the sweetest person in the world."

Ruby's eyes sparkled. "Perhaps. Regardless of her true nature, it didn't seem like enough of a motive. But then Miranda gave us a clue."

"Me?" Miranda clasped her chest as if she were on stage. "I couldn't stand the woman, but I didn't kill her."

"I wasn't accusing you," said Ruby. "You gave us insight into what drove Beryl to be so overbearing. Though she undoubtedly loved Nigel, her marriage lowered her social standing. She tried to compensate by buying new things. After that didn't work, she tried organising everyone and everything. This worked for a time, but it still wasn't enough. So what was next?"

Pixley slapped his knee. "What I write about: power and status."

"Precisely. When Fina and I first met Lady Geraldine, she mentioned her doctor asking for her vote in a local council election," said Ruby.

I tilted my head back at the grey sky. "That council meeting notice I found in Pari's garage? It sparked your curiosity."

"So that's why I had to ask a journalist friend about development plans in the local area – plans affecting Pari and Miranda directly," said Pixley.

Ruby turned towards Miranda. "You lied about the development plans, didn't you?"

Her head drooped. "Yes. But honestly, I didn't want you to get hold of the wrong end of the stick." She put a hand to her chest. "*I* knew it was irrelevant to the murder, so why confuse matters?"

"Oh, but these plans do matter," said Ruby, "because Beryl's character suggests she might have been standing for election to parliament soon."

"It's true," said Nigel quietly. "I tried to talk her out of it, but once Beryl decides something, it's impossible to shift her."

Ainsley said, "One moment. Do you have any evidence Beryl Triggs was standing for election? And even if you did, how would killing her solve the development problem for Miss Oliver or Miss Karan?"

"I can answer that," said Nigel. "Beryl had a finger in every pie in Crickle Hythe. She needn't be on the council to play a role in the plans moving forward or not."

"But if the plans did go forward, they'd probably help her win the election," said Ruby.

Whittle rubbed her lips. "A convincing theory, Miss Dove, but where's the evidence?"

Both Miranda and Pari smirked. "Hear, hear, Chief Inspector," said Pari.

Ruby turned to Whittle. "Does Miranda Oliver have a criminal record?"

Everyone gasped.

Whittle sniffed. "Not precisely, Miss Dove."

"What the devil does that mean?" asked Pixley.

"Miss Oliver was never convicted."

"Did this potential crime involve guns?" asked Ruby. "Maybe it was an accident?"

Whittle rubbed her jaw, but her jaw stayed shut.

Miranda held up a hand. "It's all right, Chief Inspector." She turned to Ruby. "How did you guess?"

"Some of us noticed your skill in handling a gun," said Ruby. "And when we spoke to you in the chemist's, you said you didn't need any more trouble from the police."

Miranda nodded slowly. "I see. Well, it's true. I'm an expert shot and love to hunt. When I was fifteen, I was hunting with a friend and I shot her accidentally. Not dead – just in the leg. But someone had overheard us quarrelling before the accident and told the police. That launched a full-scale inquiry."

"Thank you for your honesty," said Ruby. "Now we've cleared up that matter, we can focus on what actually happened. Pari, would you mind helping me?"

Pari studied Ruby warily. Then, with a little shrug, she ambled towards Ruby, her skirts floating in the breeze. "Well? Get on with it, Miss Dove."

Ruby took a step closer to Pari. "Imagine I'm the murderer and I'm holding Lady Geraldine's brooch in a handkerchief. It's dark, and Mrs Triggs is distracted. I want to convince Mrs Triggs to take the brooch and pin it to her lapel without any fuss. And remember, the only people aware of the missing brooch at this point are Nigel, Callum, Atina, Lady Geraldine, and Fina. Plus the murderer, of course."

"Why not just jab Beryl with the brooch?" asked Milo.

"Because she'd shriek," said Pari.

Ruby made a sudden jabbing motion at Pari and she leapt back, demonstrating the point.

"Let's now reverse roles, Pari," said Ruby. "You play the murderer."

I held my breath. Surely Pari wasn't the murderer, was she?

Pari rubbed her eyes. "If it will give us the bloody answer, I'll stand on my head."

"Right you are," said Ruby. "Now, let's pretend that you, Pari, have stolen the brooch, and you approach Beryl with it in your hand. What do you say to convince Beryl to take it? Especially if she realises it belongs to Lady Geraldine?"

Pari frowned and surveyed the mud, as if it might hold the answer. She glanced up again. "I have no bloody idea. If I say, 'Mrs Triggs, I found this brooch, do you want it?' she'll look at me as if I were barmy. Quite rightly, too."

"Yes, Beryl would ask questions," said Ruby.

"I certainly couldn't accidentally jab her with it."

"Yes," said Ruby. "But let's assume you do convince Beryl to take the brooch. Will she let you pin it on her?"

Pari grimaced. "It's doubtful."

"Too intimate," I said, as the truth surfaced in my brain. "You'd only pin a brooch on someone if it were a gift – a gift that wouldn't be entirely surprising. From a lover."

We all looked at each other.

Whittle ran both hands through her short hair, making it stand on end. "A lover. Are you saying Beryl Triggs had a lover?"

Poor Nigel Triggs's mouth was open again. "It-it-it can't be. It can't be."

Miranda gently rubbed his arm.

"Beryl was a searcher, like a shark," said Ruby. "Always seeking improvement, flattery, or a sign she was worthy in some way. And if a slightly younger man came along and bolstered her self-esteem, well, that was all to the good."

"Are you saying she had an affair?" asked Whittle.

"The only person who can answer is the murderer," said Ruby.

"Half a mo," said Pixley. "If Beryl wanted status, then only one man fits the bill."

"Pixley is correct, isn't he, Mr Sinclair?" said Ruby.

———

Callum lunged at Ruby, but Sergeant Ainsley flew from his seat, grabbing and shoving Callum's arms behind his back.

"You haven't any evidence," Callum said, matching Ruby's quiet but dangerous tone. "All you have is a pretty story. Besides, if your theory is correct, what about Milo Judson? He's better looking than I am, and certainly a man for the ladies."

"I left out one final detail," said Ruby. "The theft. If Milo were Mrs Triggs's lover, would she believe he'd come by that brooch in a legitimate way? Even if Mrs Triggs didn't realise it was Lady Geraldine's, she'd scarcely ignore the size of that diamond. A conversation would ensue, a luxury the murderer simply couldn't afford. Time was of the essence."

"Well," said Pixley, "the murderer couldn't risk discussing where he'd found the brooch or how he'd had enough money to buy it."

Whittle's eyebrows rose. "Wait. Are we assuming Mrs Triggs would accept such a gift from a lover right in front of her husband?"

Nigel blinked, and Miranda hugged him closer. His brain couldn't process what was happening – truly a case of shock if ever there was one.

"That's the heart of the matter," said Ruby. "The only way Mrs Triggs would accept the gift was under two conditions. One, the gift would be from a lover. And two, that the gift-giver had a legitimate claim to the brooch."

"Blow me down," said Pixley. "Callum fits the bill perfectly."

"Even if Mrs Triggs and Callum weren't romantically involved, the story still holds water. Callum gives her the brooch, saying it's a token of Lady Geraldine's appreciation for everything she's done for the gala and the village."

Whittle twitched her full lips at Callum. "What about it, Mr Sinclair?"

"I deny it. You still haven't any proof." His eyes bore into Ruby's. "And where's my motive, dear Miss Dove?"

CHAPTER
Twenty-Five

THE NEXT DAY, we found ourselves seated at Pixley's kitchen table on his cosy narrowboat. I longed to stretch out for a snooze on the velvet-cushioned bench, but he'd insisted that we sit at his table to await his surprise.

I was surprised, but not by whatever Pixley had in store for us. My disbelief stemmed from Ruby's failure to solve this case. Well, Ruby Dove hadn't exactly failed, but she hadn't succeeded either. Perhaps this Oxford rustication business had clouded her otherwise razor-sharp mind.

Ruby banged her fist, sending the cutlery jumping on the table. "I'm right. I know I'm right. Callum is the murderer."

"Here, Ruby." Pixley slid a highball with blue and green liquid across the table. "This is my surprise. Drink up and you'll feel better."

Tipping the glass back and forth, Ruby squinted at the concoction like it was one of her chemistry experiments. "What is it? Are you experimenting with poisons, too?"

He folded his hands over his belly, regarding Ruby with a complacent smile. Then he flipped open a wooden cupboard built into the side of the table, revealing neatly aligned bottles filled with colourful liquids. "Now that I own a home – or rather a narrowboat – I've taken to mixing cocktails. I call this one Ruby's Deep. You know, because you're a deep one, and it looks like the deep blue sea."

"Erm, yes, Pix." I sipped my drink, contemplating the murky flow of the canal through the window. "I must confess I'm also a bit foggy on Callum's motive, Ruby."

"All right." She folded her hands neatly in her lap. "Riddle me this: if you were madly in love with someone, would you let their clothes fall into disrepair and make them work harder than a dog – assuming you had the money to solve these two problems?"

"Absolutely not," said Pixley. "Even if I were thrifty, I wouldn't let that happen."

Ruby drummed on the table. "That's exactly what I thought when I noticed Atina's frayed sleeves. It reminded me about the general state of decay at Chidden Park. If Callum were careful with money, he might well have let the garden grow wild, but why would he force Atina to work so hard and wear tattered clothes?"

"Which means he's not her lover," I said.

"Or he's lying about the state of his bank account," said Ruby.

"Well, it's easy enough to check," said Pixley. "Ring up old Whittle and ask her to snoop around."

"I will," said Ruby. "But it's still not enough."

Pixley rose and pushed open the skylight above us, letting in a whoosh of air. "Thought I'd open the old Houdini hatch to let some air in on the subject. Maybe it will stimulate our brain cells."

Then he snapped his fingers. "I almost forgot." He opened the flap of his leather bag and withdrew an envelope.

"Have you been holding out on us, Pixley Hayford?" I asked.

He grimaced, sending his spectacles sky-high above his nose. "I swear, it wasn't intentional. When we were in Lady Geraldine's room after her disappearance, I spotted some papers in the waste bin."

Ruby busied herself with scanning the papers he handed to her, but she still had time to quip, "So you thought you'd be public-spirited and take out the rubbish for Lady Geraldine, didn't you?"

"Aye, that's the long and the short of it. Sorry."

I scooted my chair next to Ruby. "Anything useful?"

"Looks like bills, lists, and a few photos. And a letter from the bank."

She handed me each item in turn but nothing looked interesting. The photos looked to be of poor quality, which was probably why Lady Geraldine was throwing them away. One was of her as a child, petting a cat, and another was of her at the seaside with a few adults. The third was more recent, featuring a slightly younger Lady Geraldine and a woman standing behind her, though she was so short that their heads were nearly at the same level. The woman looked familiar, but I couldn't place her. Perhaps I'd seen her in other photos about the house. I flipped it over. In pencil, someone had scrawled *FW* on the back. The fourth photo featured Lady Geraldine and Callum. It looked like it was taken in the orchard. On the back of this photo, it read *CS* and *CP*.

Ruby pointed at the photo. "I presume *CS* and *CP* mean Callum Sinclair and Chidden Park. Did you notice that the dovecote isn't there?"

I nodded. "Is that significant?"

Ruby put down the bank letter. "The photos are most instructive, though I'm not yet sure how it all ties together. What *is* significant is Lady Geraldine's bank balance."

"How much?" asked Pixley.

I giggled. "You didn't even read it, Pix?"

He held up his hands in surrender. "As I told you, I forgot I'd even put them in my bag."

"Lady Geraldine had five hundred thousand pounds in the bank," said Ruby.

Pixley whistled. "More than enough motive for murder."

I swirled the blue-green liquid in my glass. "It's helpful confirmation of his motive, but it's still not evidence. Surely Callum has other skeletons stuffed into a cupboard somewhere."

Suddenly, Ruby gulped her drink and slammed down the glass. "Brilliant, Feens. Skeletons. Yes, yes! Why didn't it occur to us earlier?"

Pixley wiped a hand across his face. "I'm knackered, but not that knackered. What's this about skeletons?"

"Fina's boyfriend!" she cried. "How can we find Niall Rafferty? Will he still be at that house?"

"As much as I'd love to see Niall—"

"Wouldn't you just," Pixley said.

"Don't tease her, Pix. This is serious," said Ruby.

"I haven't the foggiest where Niall might be," I said. "It's doubtful he'd still be at the house – wouldn't he be worried the police might find him there?"

Despite my doubts, Ruby insisted on searching for Niall. So we left behind our cosy quarters and drove into the night. A tunnel of bending trees arched over the road as we approached the house. The effect ought to have been charming, but the cold moonlight only made it sinister.

Peeking over tall hedges, the white gables of the Hansel-and-Gretel house came into view. Ruby manoeuvred the car over a few humps and turned left onto the drive. As we rolled to a halt, I listened to the silence. No birds sang, and no beasties rustled in the undergrowth.

The house was dark, save a sliver of faded light somewhere in the hallway. All the curtains were drawn, and I half expected Niall to peer from one of the windows.

"I say, we should have had that Halloween bash here," said Pixley. "Most atmospheric."

I shivered. "If Niall were here, we would have heard or seen something by now. Shall we return to Pixley's narrowboat for one last nightcap?"

"Spiffing idea, Red," said Pixley.

Ruby tapped her hand on the driving wheel. "Not so fast. I say that Niall's still in the house. Shall we bet on it?"

"Is Milo rubbing off on you?" asked Pixley. "Because that way only leads to tears."

"Just a friendly wager," said Ruby. "Drinks at your favourite place."

"All right," I said. "Pix and I will split the winnings, since we're wagering Niall's not here."

We shook hands with Ruby.

"Right." She opened the door.

"Wait," said Pixley. "Shouldn't we wait until we hear something?"

"We'll be here until dawn if we do that," she said.

"Better than stumbling upon a ghostie in the haunted house," I said.

Ruby knew us too well. She simply closed the door and marched up the thick shingle carpeting the drive.

Pixley and I looked at each other, sighed, and decamped from the warmth of the motor car.

Ruby switched on her torch. "Pixley can take the downstairs and Fina and I will go upstairs."

"Aye, aye." Pixley's torch played against the wall, looking like splashed white paint over the dark exterior.

Pixley tottered into the kitchen, his torchlight jiggling wildly. Ruby kicked off her shoes and began padding up the stairs. She turned and whispered, "You take the right and I'll take the left."

She disappeared to the left, just as I crested the stairs. The only sounds were the floorboards creaking in protest and the soft metallic clunks of pots and pans coming from below.

My stockings caught on loose floorboard, making the dreaded "crrrk" sound. I was about to start cursing like Pari, but a slithering sound made me freeze on the spot.

It sounded like someone dragging a sack. A large sack.

With a deep breath, I stepped towards the closed door.

CHAPTER
Twenty-Six

THERE'S A PERFECTLY *rational explanation for that sound, Fina.*

My rational mind had fled long before I'd entered this dratted house. Only my lovely messy, emotional mind had hold of me now, spinning out every possible fantastic scenario, from anacondas escaped from the zoo to bodies being dragged across the floor.

Ruby and Pixley are here, Fina. Be calm.

So I touched the doorknob. The cold metal was a welcome sign. Niall must have left hours ago, and the slithering sound was probably a frolicking fox outside. Or maybe even a rat inside. Not that I wished to frolic with a rat at that moment, but it was definitely preferable to an anaconda or a dead body.

I twisted the knob and pushed the door, training my torchlight into the crack. Nothing was inside. Emboldened, I opened the door wide, revealing the room just as I'd left it that afternoon.

A tree branch scratched the window, sending my heart racing. Then I relaxed. That was probably the sound I'd heard before.

With a great exhale, I loosened my shoulders and returned to the corridor. I was about to call to Ruby when I stopped.

All the noises had faded. No gentle clanging from downstairs, no creaking floorboards.

No footsteps. Nothing.

Perhaps they'd already regrouped outside.

Conscious as ever of my own footsteps, I slid along the floorboards. I wanted to hear the silence over my own movements.

The staircase stood before me now, descending into a terrifying darkness. I played my torch onto it, just to remind myself it was perfectly normal.

I grabbed the banister and took the first step. An arm suddenly circled around my middle and pulled me up. I screamed and screamed as I was pulled backwards, back into the corridor and into a room.

"Fina!" came a voice, half exasperated and half commanding.

The torchlight shone on his face. It was Niall.

Now that I'd stopped screaming, I heard banging coming from below us and down the hallway.

"I had to separate you from your friends," Niall whispered. "Don't worry. They're perfectly safe – only slightly irked at being locked away."

He propped his torch on a table against the wall, creating a soft light across half his face.

"Why did you come, Fina?" His eyes darted from side to side, searching for the answer in mine.

His soft Dublin lilt was so reassuring, even as he asked such a question. Despite the blessed racket from Ruby and Pixley, I wanted to stay right here and to push away all thoughts of murder, Oxford, and what on earth I was doing with my life.

"Fina?" he said gently.

I shook myself. Time enough for gazing into his eyes at some later date. "We need evidence, Niall. We need your testimony."

He cocked his head. "You know I can't give evidence. Besides, no one would believe me – at least not at the moment."

"Niall, you can't keep running. What's the worst that'll happen if you tell the police about Cornwall?"

I couldn't see his eyes, but I didn't need to. It was a ridiculous suggestion, and yet I had a glimmer of hope that everything might be fine.

"Even if the police believed my story, I wouldn't jeopardise all those people involved in certain activities. You know which activities I mean – you and your friends are in the same position."

"Where will you go? When will we meet again?"

He brushed my cheek with the warm leather fingertips of his glove. "Fina, I—"

The headlamps of a car swung wildly across the ceiling. It was turning into the drive.

"It's the police," Niall said. "I must go."

"Wait. There must be a way to find evidence to clear your name."

He stopped halfway to the door.

"It may not help me, but it will help this case: ask the child. They'll give you what you need."

Then he rushed back towards me.

Sergeant Ainsley's cut-glass words came from outside.

"You must go before it's too late," I whispered.

He squeezed my arms and breathed into my ear. "He's spying on you. Don't let him get away with it."

Niall pressed a warm metal object into my hand and crawled out of the window.

The banging noise crescendoed downstairs, coming from Ainsley and company at the front door.

I opened my hand. For a moment, I stared at the long key as if it were a talisman, wondering if I'd ever see Niall again.

But Ainsley's yelling returned me to my sour reality. I dashed down the hall and released Ruby from her room.

Pressing the key into her hand, I gasped, "Release Pix, will you? I'll distract them at the front door until you let him out – we don't want them to know Niall was here."

We flew down the stairs and Ruby vanished into the corridor.

I yelled, "I'm coming," at the front door, seething with rage. My rage at remembering Niall's words – Ainsley must have been spying on us. All my suspicions about the blue-eyed boy had been correct.

As soon as I heard two sets of footsteps coming from the kitchen, I flung open the door, ready to punch that smug copper in the gut.

But it was the kindly face of Chief Inspector Whittle.

"Fancy meeting you here, Miss Aubrey-Havelock. And what a surprise! Miss Dove and Mr Hayford are here, too."

"Did you follow us?" I put my hands on my hips. No more fun and games. After all, they were the reason I couldn't see Niall.

"We did follow you, though we had a slow start with Mr Hayford's narrowboat. Stuck in the mud."

I said nothing.

Whittle removed her scarf, as if she were being invited in for tea. "Care to explain what you've been up to?"

Ainsley's face popped over Whittle's shoulder. "And why you find this house so fascinating?"

Ruby stepped into the breech. "We're as desperate for evidence as you are, Chief Inspector. Perhaps we missed something."

Whittle twisted her lips to the side, saying nothing whilst saying everything at the same time. It's true that our actions must have seemed bizarre to her.

Pixley stepped forward. "Look here, Chief Inspector. We believed Callum would need a place away from Chidden Park to plan his crime."

He waved his hand about, as if he were an estate agent showing a promising property. "This charming house is brimming with character and—"

"What Pixley means is Callum needed a place away from prying village eyes to concoct his scheme. So he came here and we thought we'd find evidence of that," said Ruby.

Sergeant Ainsley made a tsk-ing sound with his teeth.

I had to do something, and although I didn't want to share Niall's insights with the police, the situation was becoming desperate. "Chief Inspector, we believe one of the children at the gala saw something. Something that will lead us to evidence."

Everyone stared at me.

I shrugged. "It occurred to me a few moments ago. We only asked Archie about that night, but we didn't ask Etty. She might have spotted the murderer but didn't know it."

CHAPTER
Twenty-Seven

SQUINTING IN THE MORNING SUN, I edged my chair away from the herb-covered window of Pari's cottage. Whilst the warmth was welcome, my lack of sleep made me feel like a vampire desperate to avoid the light.

I sipped my strong tea, eagerly awaiting the arrival of biscuits.

Pari rattled the biscuit tin. "Sorry, Fina. We're fresh out of biscuits."

I pasted a smile on my face to cover a grimace. She hadn't any milk, either, so I hoped the acid of the tea wouldn't turn my already jumpy stomach.

Ruby leaned back in her chair. "Sorry to disturb you so early, Miss Karan, but we thought you'd like the chance to explain yourself before the police arrive."

Pari's head snapped up. "What the devil? Explain myself about what?"

"Why were you searching Mrs Triggs's coat on the night of the gala? Perhaps you were putting the brooch in her pocket?"

"Tommyrot. You're talking gibberish."

A car pulled up outside.

"It might be the police," said Ruby. "Would you prefer to explain it to them?"

Pari whipped the worktop with her dishcloth. "Damn and blast it."

But then her shoulders drooped, and she collapsed onto a nearby chair. She spoke quietly, something I thought she couldn't do. "Beryl said Miranda and Milo were having an affair. She said she'd give me the evidence at the gala."

"Did she want money for her information?" asked Ruby.

"No. She liked to have power over people. I suspect that gossipy husband of hers supplied the details."

"Did you find anything in Mrs Triggs's coat?" asked Ruby.

"No."

Miranda burst through the door. "Hello, people. Pari, I've brought you your favourite shortbread."

"Thanks, love." Pari stared intently at a radiator.

Miranda set the tin on the crowded worktop. "Why's everyone so glum?"

With uncharacteristic bluntness, Ruby asked, "Were you having an affair, Miranda?"

"With whom?" Miranda munched a biscuit as if Ruby had simply asked her the time of day.

Pari buried her face in her hands. "My lovely idiot, you've just admitted to it. If you weren't having any affair, you would have said, 'What the bloody hell are you talking about, woman?'!"

Miranda licked her lips and gazed out the window.

"As I was saying to Pari, time is of the essence," said Ruby. "We thought you were the police – when you pulled up on the drive."

Miranda sighed. "I'd better tell you, then. I *was* having an affair with Callum. And I broke it off just now. It was such a mistake. I'm so sorry, Pari. I simply lost my head."

Pari's eyes glistened. "You didn't have an affair with Milo?"

"Milo? Whatever gave you that idea?"

"I overheard you speaking to Milo the night of the gala," I said. "You were very close."

Miranda gave me a watery smile. "We were planning a surprise birthday party for Pari at the pub."

Pari let out a little yelp, either from surprise or pain. Perhaps it was a bit of both.

Miranda threw her arms around Pari. Pari didn't move away, but she didn't reciprocate, either.

Our little trio pretended to be fascinated by the bird in the window.

Another car rolled up outside. This time, I spotted Sergeant Ainsley's blond head.

"Good morning," came Chief Inspector Whittle's voice from the doorway. "Miss Karan, would you wake your daughter, please?"

Whittle stood with her hands clasped across her midsection, a strangely menacing pose.

"I don't want to wake Etty," said Pari. "And I'd rather not have her talk to the police, if it's all the same to you."

"I'm afraid it's not a matter of preference," said Whittle. "Please wake your daughter."

Pari let the kettle clang on the stove and stomped upstairs.

Ruby stirred her tea absently, whilst Pixley drummed on the table. I glared at Ainsley, willing him to shrivel and disappear. But not before I confronted him about spying on us – whatever that might mean. It might be because of our political activities, or maybe even for being rusticated by that evil toad named Miss Datchworth.

Whittle leaned against the kitchen table. "You'll be glad to know, Miss Dove, that your suspicion about Mr Sinclair's finances proved correct. He *was* wealthy at one time, but it's no longer the case."

"Which supplies a strong motive to kill Lady Geraldine," Ruby said. "Though we still need evidence about the Triggs murder."

Etty shuffled in, rubbing her eyes. "Yes, Mrs Chief Inspector?"

Though Whittle wasn't much taller than Etty, she crouched down to speak to her.

Etty eyed Whittle warily, seemingly interpreting her movements as condescending rather than inviting.

Sensing this, Whittle straightened and directed Etty to a chair.

"I expect your mum told you what this is about," said Whittle.

"You want to know who killed Mrs Triggs. And Lady Geraldine."

"Correct. And to find out, we want to hear about the time you spent upstairs during the Halloween party. When did you go upstairs, and what were you doing?"

"The other children were tiresome," Etty said in a would-be grown-up way. "So I took my book upstairs to find a quiet place to read. It's a smashing pirate adventure book."

"And when was this?"

She squinted at the ceiling. "Mm … rather early. A few people had arrived, but the music on the gramophone hadn't started. And Lady Geraldine was being taken down in the lift as I was coming upstairs. Mr Callum was helping her."

"And where did you go upstairs?"

"I looked in all the rooms, but I didn't go in any of them."

"Are you sure?"

She pushed her toe onto the floor. "Quite sure."

Whittle hitched her chair forward. "Now, think carefully. Did you notice anyone in them?"

She shook her head. Then she squinted again. "Except for the jester."

My stomach lurched, remembering Nigel traipsing down the stairs, jingling in his jester costume. Was Ruby wrong about Callum? Was it Nigel all along?

"But the jester had only gone to the toilet," put in Etty. "I noticed him go in and then go out."

"Did you see the large bedroom?" asked Whittle. "The one belonging to Lady Geraldine?"

"Yes."

"Was the door open?"

"Yes."

"So you saw no one, apart from the jester."

"When I came down the stairs, I saw her."

Etty pointed at me, sending my face flaming.

"Why are you blushing, Miss Aubrey-Havelock?" asked Ainsley.

"Because I'm embarrassed by my ridiculous fancy dress, Sergeant."

"You went into the room to change, Miss Aubrey-Havelock, so between that moment and the lights going off, someone could have stolen the brooch," said Whittle.

Etty swung her legs, starting to enjoy the proceedings. "Except that I went back upstairs and sat on the landing with some cushions I'd found downstairs."

"Why did you do that?" asked Whittle.

"I told you. I wanted a place to read, and those rooms smelled peculiar. So I sat near the stairs until the lights went out."

"Did anyone use the lift?"

Etty stared at us blankly, the way a child does when an adult says something stupid. "Of course not. It was locked after Mr Sinclair helped Lady Geraldine into it."

Ruby bit her lip. "There's your evidence, Chief Inspector. You have two witnesses saying no one came in or out of that room after Lady Geraldine had gone down in the lift and before Fina discovered that the brooch had been stolen. The murderer must be Callum or Atina, and we've already established why Atina would not be the person to give Mrs Triggs the brooch."

Suddenly, a wave of nausea arose from my throat. "The tea!" I spluttered, running from the room. I knew it probably looked like I was pretending, but this was a genuine emergency.

"She's not been poisoned, has she?" I heard Pari call from the kitchen.

Reassuring murmurs arose from Pixley and Ruby as I slammed the door to the toilet. After a few quality moments with the washbasin, I breathed more easily. I should have asked for a piece of toast. I knew tea without milk on an empty stomach was a daft idea.

Now with a light spring in my step, I moved towards the welcome smells of toast and butter in the kitchen. Pari must have read my mind.

As I passed a room with the door ajar, I heard Sergeant Ainsley's voice. It sounded like he was telephoning someone.

"Yes, sir." Pause. "It's been very convenient they've been so involved in the case. It's been much easier to keep an eye on them. Yes, Whittle's been a great asset."

In a sudden fury, I kicked open the door.

The telephone receiver fell through Ainsley's long fingers with a clunk onto the floor.

Before he could lean over to pick it up, I'd dashed to his side and scooped it up.

"Hello. Hello," I said. "Whomever you are, Sergeant Ainsley is an ass. He knows nothing and will never know anything. We know you've been following us, and I hope you rot in hell."

I looked up.

A crowd had formed in the doorway, with faces ranging from the puzzled Whittle to the triumphant Ruby and Pixley.

Pixley clapped. "Well done, Fina. Well done."

Ruby strode forward, coming an inch from Sergeant Ainsley's nose. "Who are you really working for? The Secret Intelligence Service?"

"What's this about, Sheridan?" Whittle's face had turned from puzzled to a frown. "Who were you speaking to on the telephone?"

"A colleague in Yorkshire, ma'am. We were constables together, and I was updating him on the case."

"That's not what it sounded like to me," I said.

Ainsley said nothing.

As satisfied as I felt, I knew this was a losing battle. Neither Whittle nor Ainsley would admit anything in front of us all. Even if Whittle were truly surprised, she'd still close ranks.

Ruby stood back, surveying Ainsley as if he were a particularly despicable individual. I had to agree.

"Well, at least we know who to watch," said Ruby. "Don't think I wasn't aware we were being followed. And if Miss Datchworth of Quenby College is also part of your inner circle, Sergeant Ainsley, tell her that when the principal returns, we're going to request an inquiry of our own."

Ainsley snorted. "I don't know what you're rabbiting on about, but remember that I'm a police officer."

Pixley stepped forward, also coming within an inch of Ainsley – though given Pixley's height, he was within an inch of his chest rather than his nose. "And remember, I'm a journalist. I don't have the connections you have, but I certainly have friends who owe me favours. And the old cliché is true: the pen is mightier than the sword."

Pari broke out in spontaneous applause. "Perfectly marvellous, absolutely bloody marvellous. What a show!"

CHAPTER
Twenty-Eight

TWO WEEKS LATER, I found myself staring again at Miss Toad – or rather, Miss Datchworth. Truly, it was as if the past month was simply a dream – or a nightmare, depending on your perspective.

Her pale pink tongue delicately traced the outer edge of her lips. Not that she had any lips to speak of.

In an unusual show of discomfort, Ruby visibly drew back in her chair, shivering involuntarily. A shaft of light dared to peak through the heavy curtains of the office, highlighting clouds of dust and Miss Datchworth's ghostlike appearance.

Ruby removed her tight leather gloves, one finger at a time. This provocation forced Miss Datchworth to look up from her stack of papers, a sheaf of yellowing brittle pages so old they might have been penned by Charles Dickens. Or maybe Mary Shelley was a more appropriate reference.

With a rasping wheeze, Miss Datchworth deigned us with her full attention, bulging eyes and all. "I would normally say it's a pleasure to see you, Miss Dove, but under the circumstances let's forgo that little formality, shall we?"

Ruby graced her with a tight smile.

"And Miss Aubrey-Havelock, I cannot say it is a pleasure to see you again, either."

"The feeling is mutual, Miss Datchworth."

Out of the corner of my eye, I saw Ruby grimace.

But Miss Datchworth surprised me with another wheeze. This time, I think it was a chuckle. "Ah, a girl with spirit. Well, I must say we aim to channel that spirit in a healthier way here at Quenby. But nevertheless, I'm glad to see you have it."

Ruby leaned forward. "Miss Datchworth, your time is valuable, and—"

"That it is, Miss Dove, that it is. So I will come to the point. After reviewing your case over the past few weeks, I've decided that—"

The door burst open and Principal Laverton strode in.

Miss Datchworth rose, every inch of her personality transformed from an odious toad into a simpering stoat.

"Principal!" Miss Datchworth shuffled papers on her desk. "What a pleasant surprise, I'm sure. We didn't expect your return for another week. Is anything the matter?"

I'd only seen the principal a few times, striding across the lawn in a long brown cassock-like dress. She had keys cinched to her belt like a monk's get-up. Up close, she had smooth and unlined pale skin, even though she must be nearing sixty.

"Nothing is the matter, Miss Datchworth. I simply had to return to work – all this lying about is well and good, but I've finally come to accept that I'm not like that. My brain demands action."

"Oh, of course, Principal, of course," Miss Datchworth said.

The principal removed her tiny round spectacles and blew on them. "Now, tell me what's happening here, Miss Datchworth. I believe, yes, you're Miss Dove and Miss Aubrey-Havelock, aren't you?"

She peered at each of us in turn, like we were newly discovered algae specimens under the microscope. "Yes. Miss Dove, I've heard of you – not only about that Cornwall business, mind you, but from your chemistry tutor. We need more women in chemistry, Miss Dove."

"Yes, Principal. Thank you," said Ruby, clearly as much in awe of Principal Laverton as I was.

"And Miss Aubrey-Havelock, yes …" She rubbed her chin. "I've heard you cause a spot of trouble here and there, but you have a first-class analytical mind."

"Me? Analytical? Oh no, you must mean Ruby."

Ruby gave me an exasperated look.

The principal shook her head. "No, I'm positive one of your history tutors told me that, and they're never wrong, are they?"

"No, Principal. Never," I said, finally realising I ought to accept the compliment gracefully.

She slid her glasses back on her nose and walked over to the desk, looming over Miss Datchworth. "Now, tell me why these two fine young ladies are in your room, Lavinia. Giving them much deserved praise, are you?"

It wasn't a question. It was an assumption.

Ruby and I exchanged quick, hopeful glances.

"Well, we, I mean, I—"

"That's settled then, isn't it?" The principal glanced up at us. "Thank you, Miss Dove and Miss Aubrey-Havelock. Thank you for being so attentive to the world at large. I'm quite sure it feels you're undervalued, but please remember that we here at Quenby do value your contributions and continued hard work in pursuit of knowledge. That will be all."

"Yes, Principal," we said together.

Then Ruby and I jumped up, fleeing the room before she changed her mind.

Outside Miss Datchworth's rooms, we scurried down the long hall, our shoes making a terrible racket against the ancient stone floor.

"What did the principal mean by being 'attentive to the world at large'?" I asked. "Surely she cannot be aware of our political activities. Although Miss Datchworth looked like she was going to croak."

Ruby stopped. "Croak. Yes, looked like she was going to croak." She squeezed my arms. "You've done it, Feens. You've done it!"

I stared, open-mouthed. A flood of students pushed around us, giggling at us and rushing away.

As their footsteps faded into the distance, I searched Ruby's face for a sign of what she meant. But all I received in return was tooth-tapping, although that was unsurprising if she'd had a revelation.

"Are you going to tell me why my observation about Miss Datchworth was so brilliant?" I asked.

"Mmm …"

"There you are!"

The figure of Pixley Hayford in a green plaid tweed suit hurried towards us. "You've been ages! What's the word on the street? Did that Datchworth creature give as good as she got?"

He looked at me and then at Ruby. "Must be dashed bad news if you forgot I was sitting on that dratted bench outside, fending off raindrops. And potential suitors, of course."

"Ruby is thinking, Pix," I hissed.

He silently blinked his understanding like morse code.

With a gentle nudge, he urged me towards two ancient high-backed chairs, the kind that looked like precursors to some mediaeval torture.

We sat on the hard wood, watching Ruby still standing in the middle of the corridor. At least she was contemplating the light streaming through the stained-glass windows now.

"Whilst we're waiting for Sherlock Dove's epiphany, I have my own revelation. Well, perhaps that's too strong a word. Maybe serendipity? No—"

I put a hand on his arm. "Just tell me, Pix."

"Right-o. As I said, I was waiting on that bench outside, fighting off the raindrops and incipient autumn chill, when who do you think came striding across the emerald-green quad of your eminent college?"

"Surprise me, Pix." The last few days, no, scratch that – the last few weeks had been positively exhausting. I was in no mood for fun and games.

"My, you are tetchy, aren't you? I'm sorry I don't have a snack stored in my pockets. Must be low blood sugar again."

"Pix." My hand turned into a fist in my lap.

"Steady on, Red. All right. I'll take you and Ruby to a slap-up lunch at the Ritz if we can solve all this funny business at Crickle Hythe. It will make a stupendous story."

Blast it, he was right. I was hungry. But I also wanted to solve this 'funny business' of Crickle Hythe, too. Especially now that we'd averted the dual disaster of Miss Datchworth and rustication.

"Go on."

He pulled up a trouser leg and leaned forward. "Atina Kattos was the one walking through the quad."

"So?"

His face fell like a soufflé. "So? What's she doing at Quenby College?"

"Search me," I said. "But she did say she wanted to return to Oxford to continue her studies, remember?"

"Precisely," he said. "The point being that she hadn't a bean."

"Maybe she's on scholarship," I said.

His forehead wrinkled. "You mean she secured a scholarship in the last two weeks? Seems doubtful, Red, even if she is some sort of mad genius."

Feeling defensive, I said, "Well, she could have been visiting a friend."

Pixley snapped his fingers. "Look!"

Atina Kattos strode across the quad, hair flapping in the wind.

Her confident gait and posture suggested that Quenby was her home.

I scrabbled to my feet and shot off across the wet grass of the quad. "Atina! Atina!" I called.

Such drama was probably unnecessary, but I wasn't exactly myself at that moment.

She whipped around and stopped. A bizarre smirk creased half of her face. "Fina. How delightful to see you," she said, as if she were a lady deigning to see a peasant.

As I caught my breath, Pixley trotted towards us with Ruby in tow.

"I just, I just—" I pretended I was winded, playing for time. I only knew I had to stop her in her tracks, but I hadn't a clue what to do with her now.

"Ah, Miss Kattos," said Pixley, holding out a hand. "Good to see you. I'm working on a story about what it's like to be a student here at Oxford – from a lady's perspective. Mind if I interview you as well?"

She graced us with a bitter laugh. "Dear Mr Hayford, I'm not a student here."

Ruby cocked her head. "Really? You seemed so at home here as you walked across the quad."

Atina gave us that smirk again. "Ever the detective, aren't you, Ruby? Well, it's true that I hope to be a student here very soon. I was planning to speak to a Miss Datchworth about it since I heard the principal wasn't available."

"Fortunately, Principal Laverton has just returned," said Ruby. "But I'm curious about what's changed for you."

"Changed?"

"What Ruby means is where did you find the money to pay for Oxford fees? Did you receive a scholarship?" I asked.

"I forgot how direct you are, Fina." She flung back her head. "No scholarship. But I have come into a bit of money."

"From Mr Sinclair?" asked Pixley.

"Yes, but it's not what you think."

"Oh?" asked Pixley.

She let out a stream of words. "I suppose it doesn't matter now – Callum and I are in love, yes, but that's not why he gave me the money. He's, he's—"

"Callum is dying, isn't he?" Ruby asked quietly.

CHAPTER
Twenty-Nine

ALL THREE OF us stared open-mouthed at Ruby. Even people rushing through the quad stopped to gawp at us.

"But how did you know?" asked Atina. "I thought Callum hid it so well."

"He did, or rather, he does," said Ruby. "But it was the register at the chemist's that first put the idea in my mind."

The image of the book popped into my mind's eye. "The only thing Callum bought was throat lozenges. And so did Nigel."

"Dear Feens has such an excellent memory."

"Thank you for the compliment, but I still don't see why throat lozenges make you think Callum is dying," I said.

"He bought five boxes, whilst Nigel bought one."

"So?" I queried.

"It seemed significant to me. But none of this was in my conscious mind until Fina drew it to the surface a few minutes ago."

"How?" I lifted my head to the sky for the answer. "When I said 'croak'? But surely that didn't mean he was going to die."

"Because 'croak' had two meanings when you said it, that's what allowed the pieces to fall into place," said Ruby. "Remember how raspy Callum's voice is? That kind of voice usually comes from smoking many cigarettes for many years, but I never saw him smoke."

I remembered asking Callum for a cigarette when he caught me in Lady Geraldine's room.

"And he was strangely out of breath when we climbed the stairs together," she continued. "On top of that, when we were discussing the murder with Atina and Callum earlier, do you recall Atina lighting up and then hurriedly putting out her cigarette?"

"I thought she was just nervous," said Pixley.

"The other notable detail was Callum's dwindling weight. Did you notice how thin he was?"

"True," I said. "But I didn't have a point of reference to begin with. And he seemed worried in general, so I attributed it to a loss of appetite due to worry."

"Ah, if only Red and I had that problem," said Pixley. "Though I never worry."

Then he looked abashed at his rare misstep. "Sorry. I shouldn't have said that."

Ruby ploughed ahead. "So when Fina said 'croak', I remembered an uncle of mine who had throat cancer. Same symptoms. Now, it could be that the symptoms were caused by other, less sinister causes, such as a cold and chronic worry, but why was he so worried?"

Wiping away a tear, Atina nodded. "The doctors gave him six months at the most."

After a respectful silence, Pixley said, "If that's true, then why would Callum commit murder for money?"

"He did it for love, didn't he?" asked Ruby.

Atina's tears were flowing now. "The fool wanted me to have the money, and he knew the only way was to kill Lady Geraldine. Though I'd never condone what he did, it was a sort of mercy because her mind and body were failing so rapidly. She'd been a fierce lady her whole life, but what you witnessed was a mask – a mask to keep her going by sheer determination. Her anger was directed at her body and mind, even though she took it out on those around her."

"And Beryl? Beryl knew about Callum's cancer diagnosis, didn't she?"

Atina's eyes blazed. "That stupid tart was going to tell her gossiping husband and the whole world about his cancer."

Almost to herself, Ruby said, "So Callum's plan was to kill his aunt, but when Beryl threatened to expose his motive – even before the crime – he had to silence her."

Pixley adjusted his spectacles. "I'm a city man myself, but even I'm aware of how foolhardy Callum would be to try and keep his illness a secret in a village full of gossips."

The only response was one fat teardrop rolling down Atina's cheek.

I put a hand on Atina's arm. "He probably wasn't himself, was he? After the diagnosis, I mean."

She blew her nose into a handkerchief, shaking her head like a wet dog. "He went a little mad, I suppose. I can't say I blame him – how would any of us react if we discovered we had six months to live?"

I bit my tongue. Whilst I empathised – or tried to empathise – murder would probably be the furthest thing from my mind in such a situation.

"You know," said Pixley, "in a rather rum way, it does him credit. Not that I approve of murder, of course, but to be so focused on finding money for you, Atina. It's touching."

She looked down at her shoes.

"I agree with you, Pix, but it still doesn't justify murder," said Ruby.

With sudden alarm, Atina glanced up from her handkerchief. "You're not – you're not going to tell the police, are you?"

Ruby bit her lip. "I'm uncertain what to do." She looked at Pixley and then at me, clearly searching for guidance.

Before either of us said anything, Atina's face creased into a grotesque parody of one of the mocking gargoyles on the building behind her.

"I'll make it simple for all of you. If you go to the police, I'm afraid I'll have to tell them about your activities."

"What do you mean?" Pixley said, a little too loudly.

"Wait, Pix," said Ruby. "Go on, Atina. Tell us exactly what you plan to do if we tell the police."

Her face relaxed, moving from anger to a sort of confusion. "Plan? What plan?"

"Will you march into any old police station and denounce us as spies? Not that there's a word of truth in it, mind you."

Atina snorted. "I don't need evidence. That tired English expression 'no smoke without fire' will do quite nicely. No, I'll just tell Whittle. I'm sure the police have enough crackpots walking into stations making all kinds of denouncements."

"Interesting," said Ruby. "So you'll tell Whittle, will you?"

"Half a mo," said Pixley. "I get the part about not wanting to appear like a crackpot, but why would you go to Whittle? Surely it will make her suspicious of you – the accusation itself will seem self-serving."

Atina stepped forward. "I must go. I have things to see to."

Ruby's hand came down on her shoulder as if she were a police officer herself. "I don't think so, Atina. You'll tell us exactly why you plan to tell Whittle, right now."

She jerked herself free. "I'll do no such thing." She took a few steps forward, but Pixley blocked her way.

"If you don't tell us, we'll tell Whittle about the arrangement you two had," said Ruby. "Or rather, still have."

Atina stopped in her tracks, but she didn't look back.

Then she stiffened and spun around.

"What arrangement?"

Her mobile face had changed again this time. But it was neither the childish gargoyle nor ingenious innocent. It was cool and collected.

"So it's true, isn't it?" Ruby worked her jaw. She was absolutely furious with Atina. "You were playing nurse at Chidden Park, weren't you?"

"Look up my credentials – I'm a registered nurse."

"You may very well be, and I'm sure you had to be trained to actually care for Lady Geraldine. But it provided a convenient cover for the real reason you were there."

Pixley grasped my hand, tight, as if we were descending on a big wheel. "Good Gad," he breathed. "Was she working for Whittle, Ruby?"

"Yes, Pix. She was a police spy."

"But how? And why?" I burbled.

"It's even worse than that." Ruby rocked on her heels. "I've been such a fool. Atina Kattos murdered Beryl Triggs and Lady Geraldine."

CHAPTER
Thirty

"SHE'S RUN FOR IT!" cried Pixley.

Atina was halfway across the quad, sprinting towards the archway. Pixley flew after her like an avenging angel with strong wings. Ruby and I stood in awe at the sight – neither of us had watched Pixley run before, his legs pumping and arms perfectly positioned.

I slipped off my shoes, ready to follow in his footsteps. Ruby put a hand on me and pointed towards the large window overlooking the quad. Miss Datchworth and the principal stood surveying the scene.

"We can't catch her up anyway," said Ruby. "And the last thing we need is a shoeless Fina dashing across the quad like the madwoman we know and love so well."

"I'm not mad," I said in a huff, even as I slipped my shoes back on. "But we do need to be the soul of propriety in front of Datchworth and Laverton."

We walked quickly out of sight of our watchers, through the archway and onto the earthen path leading along the Cherwell. The river was high, burbling and boiling as if it were heated from beneath.

I turned back, eyeing Ruby. "So what now? Even if Pixley catches Atina, is he going to march her into the station? Should we find Whittle, hoping that scurrilous Ainsley has been transferred?"

Ruby sat on a bench and patted it. "We wait for Pixley. At the rate he was going, he will have caught her by now and will probably bring her back here."

"But how will he make her? He doesn't have handcuffs or anything – she'll probably punch him in the gut!"

"Feens!" Ruby hissed suddenly. "Get down! Behind that hideous statue of Cecil Rhodes."

I did as I was told. Ruby did the same, behind a statue of Cervantes. She mouthed a word at me that I couldn't make out. So I shook my head. She grimaced and did it again, this time moving her lips into a whistling position. I still couldn't understand.

Then she picked up a twig and began moving one hand back and forth over the twig. Finally, my brain kicked into gear. It was Whittle!

I nodded my understanding, but then furrowed my brow to signal puzzlement. Why were we hiding from Whittle? Shouldn't we welcome the opportunity to tell her about our discovery?

A pigeon eyed me suspiciously, scandalised that I had lowered myself to his level.

Ruby popped up like the proverbial weasel behind the Cervantes statue and then waved me on without looking back. I straightened up and dashed after her, weaving between another flood of oncoming students.

Whilst Whittle wasn't exactly running, she was moving fast with little quick half-steps across the quad, up the stairs, and then disappearing to the right behind the bleached pillars of the chemistry building.

"Where is she going?" I breathed behind Ruby. "To test out a poison theory in the chemistry lab? And how did she slip past the porter at the lodge?"

"She's a copper, remember? All she has to do is flash her badge at the porter. The chemistry lab is often open since so many students come through. The porter tries to remind them to lock it behind them, but they never do."

The long chemistry lab was dark as all the curtains had been drawn, presumably to avoid liquids being heated by the frequently absent English sun. At the far end, I spotted a flicker of a torch. Or maybe it was a cigarette.

Ruby slid her hand along the wall and pressed a switch. The room was bathed in a pale light, revealing a forest of glass test tubes, beakers, and gleaming chrome stoves. Though I wasn't keen on chemistry myself, I suddenly understood the appeal it had for Ruby – mixing and experimenting with potions, just like she did with clothes.

"I wouldn't light a cigarette in here, Chief Inspector," called Ruby.

Whittle shaded her eyes in the light, squinting. "Ah, Ruby and Fina."

She blew a smoke ring into the air.

As if she were edging towards an explosive, Ruby put one foot forward. "I'm serious, Chief Inspector. We'll all go up in smoke if you keep puffing away."

Whittle withdrew the cigarette and made as if to throw it on the floor. Then she waved it in the air, still smiling. This wasn't her auntie smile, though. It was a superior, evil grin.

Ruby and I took another step forward.

The warmth melted from Whittle's face. "Not another step forward, if you please."

"All right," said Ruby. "Just tell us what you're doing here."

"Waiting for a lab report, naturally." Suddenly, she bent over in peals of laughter, as if this were a private joke she was sharing with an invisible colleague.

"You're here to meet Atina Kattos, aren't you?" asked Ruby.

Whittle ground the cigarette into a metal tray.

"Police business," said Whittle.

"I'll bet," said Ruby. "Police business is correct. This whole affair was police business, wasn't it?"

"You're boring me, Miss Dove. If you plan to assemble the suspects like you did last time at Chidden Park, I'm afraid that won't work. No one is here to listen to your blathering except your little sidekick poodle here."

Ruby held out a hand to bar me from moving forward. She knew me so well.

"Apologies for boring you, but I believe you'll find what I have in my pocket to be quite intriguing."

She patted her dress pocket.

"Oh?" Whittle stared at a glass tube with green liquid, as if it held the secrets of the universe.

Ruby withdrew a folded, worn piece of paper. "I've been to Somerset House recently to do a bit of research on everyone in the case. Whilst flipping through the records, I remembered that Callum's wife was named Fina."

Whittle was definitely intrigued now, though she still feigned boredom by staring out the window. I was also intrigued – and when had Ruby had time to go to Somerset House? The only time we'd been apart was when she'd been arrested and I'd been kidnapped by Niall.

Looking down at her nails, Whittle asked, "How did you know Callum's wife was called Fina?"

"Lady Geraldine told me at the gala when she remembered that my name was Fina," I said.

I glanced at Ruby, trying to fathom what I should say next. She tilted her head towards me, encouraging me to keep talking.

So I continued. "When Ruby found out, she decided to research Callum's estranged wife."

"Correct," said Ruby. "And guess what I found, Chief Inspector Alfreda Whittle?"

"Dazzle me with your brilliance, Miss Dove."

Ruby unfolded the paper. "Fina Sinclair, née Fina Whittle. You were both born in Berwick-upon-Tweed. Whittle is a name commonly found in Northumberland. And not coincidentally, it's near Scotland."

A bubble of astonishment arose in my throat, but I suppressed it. It wouldn't do to show my surprise.

"Are you saying I'm related to Callum's wife?"

"Most assuredly, Chief Inspector. You're her sister."

CHAPTER
Thirty-One

THE CHIEF INSPECTOR'S eyes fluttered at Ruby's revelation, but she said nothing.

Ruby waved the paper at Whittle, taunting her like a red rag to a bull. "It's always the little things that give away the murderer, isn't it, Chief Inspector? That night we met you, I noticed three things. First was the contrast between you and Sergeant Ainsley. We wondered why he was in the police with his obvious upper-class origins, but we didn't ask the same question of you. Why had you moved so far from your home? Your northern accent was quite strong."

Whittle snorted. "People move around all the time, Miss Dove."

"Second, I wondered why you seemed so determined to ask us questions about Callum Sinclair so soon after the murder of Beryl Triggs. Detailed questions. Hostile questions."

"It was his house. It was routine procedure."

"Third," Ruby continued, ignoring Whittle's denials, "was the fact that Scotland Yard hadn't been called in on the case. You seemed determined to have it for yourself. But why? A woman dies under mysterious circumstances at a festive gala at a manor house? Surely Scotland Yard would be called in under such circumstances."

Whittle rubbed her eye. "I'm still bored, Miss Dove. None of this adds up to anything."

"What put it all into place was the photo."

She looked up. "What photo?"

"Pixley kindly supplied us with photos taken from Lady Geraldine's waste bin. On the back of one featuring Lady Geraldine and another short, rather stocky woman, it read '*FW*'."

"I thought she looked familiar," I said, "but the initials didn't make sense. I guessed she might have been Callum's wife, Fina, but then she would have been '*FS*' for 'Fina Sinclair'."

I stopped, the obvious answer finally hitting me. "Unless it was her maiden name!"

"Fina Whittle," said Ruby quietly. "She looked remarkably similar in build to Chief Inspector Whittle. And then I remembered a conversation Fina, Pixley, and I had before the gala on that fateful night. We'd been discussing why I didn't have a nickname, whilst Fina had two. When I pondered the initials '*FW*', it struck me that 'Alfreda' could be shortened to 'Alfie' or even to *'Freda'*, which starts with an 'F'. That thought made me look at that photo a bit differently, but I'm not sure I would have ever placed her had it not been for Atina's help."

"Because Atina killed her," said Whittle flatly.

"No, not because of that," said Ruby. "Because she told us a story about her sister dying suddenly, and how she felt she had to carry on for her."

"A coincidence, I assure you."

"Perhaps, but I found it peculiar that she was sharing the story with us," said Ruby. "Why did she tell us all that?"

"Do you think she was giving us a hint?" I asked.

"Possibly," said Ruby. "Perhaps it was just her subconscious, looking for some way to communicate with us. To put us on the right track."

Whittle said nothing, but moved slowly backwards towards

the door. I couldn't stop her, as acres of test tubes and glass stood between us and her.

Unperturbed, Ruby continued. "We also discovered that Fina Whittle died a few months ago. She took her own life, didn't she? And you blamed Callum for ruining her life. That's why you took on this case, even though Scotland Yard would have wanted to investigate."

Whittle reached her hand behind her, trying to find the door handle but unable to look away from us.

Ruby took a step forward, as if she were draining away Whittle's confidence in order to feed her own. "You planned this all, didn't you? After your sister died, you blamed Callum for her death. You wanted revenge. So you searched for a way into his life. Atina Kattos proved a convenient target for your schemes. Callum was obviously in love with her, and she was vulnerable in all sorts of ways. What was it? Did you offer her money? Did you convince her that Callum would leave her money? Or did you trump up some false charge against her, threatening her?"

The door behind Whittle opened ever so slightly.

Ruby took another step forward. "That's it, isn't it? Money wasn't enough for Atina, precisely because she would likely marry Callum either before or after Lady Geraldine died of natural causes."

Whittle snorted. "Atina Kattos is a ruthless killer. She made it seem like Callum had done it, knowing full well she'd get his money."

The door opened wider, and a hand reached through it, stretching towards Whittle.

I knew that hand. Or rather, I knew that frayed sleeve.

The door flung open and Atina Kattos grabbed Whittle's arm, pulling her backwards into the darkness.

Whittle screamed and Atina clapped her hand over her mouth. Even I realised this was a foolish move. Whittle bit Atina's hand, sending Atina careening backwards into the darkness.

There was a dull thud and then quiet.

Ruby and I rushed to the door, looking around wildly for a source of light. A flash of fire lit the staircase before going dark again.

"Blasted lighter," came a familiar voice.

"Pix!" I breathed. "Where's the light?"

Someone found a switch and illuminated our pathetic scene. Pixley's jacket sat askew, and his shirt was torn. Atina's breath came in little puffs like a trapped animal, whilst Whittle lay on the floor like a sleeping dormouse.

"Did you hit Whittle over the head?" I asked Pixley.

"Had to. After dashing after Atina, I realised the futility of the exercise. What would I do with her once I 'caught' her, as it were? So I followed her here, up the staircase."

"So you heard everything," I said.

"Oh yes. And more importantly, Atina heard everything."

Atina was still breathing hard, but she held the banister, steadying herself and her breath.

"Whittle made me do it," she rasped.

"Made you kill Mrs Triggs?" asked Ruby. "And Lady Geraldine?"

Her eyes moved back and forth, searching ours. Then she sighed. "Yes. She made me kill them."

"For the money?" I asked, trying and failing to smooth the hard edges from the question.

Atina's brows furrowed. "Money? You believe I killed them for money?" Her voice rose. "You believe Whittle, then? I ought to have known you'd take sides with her, though I'm surprised you two would." She pointed at Pixley and Ruby.

"Whittle threatened you. Or threatened a loved one?" asked Ruby quietly.

"When I met this so-called chief inspector for the first time, I was impressed and put at ease. I was impressed because she was a woman in the police force, and I was put at ease by her manner – like one of my aunties back home."

"So you confided in her, didn't you?" asked Pixley.

"Like a fool, I did. I completely forgot she was a policewoman. She came to Crickle Hythe a month or so after I'd started working at Chidden Park, and she kindly took me to have tea. I told her all about my family in Cyprus and my dream of returning to Oxford."

Atina leaned against the banister. "I thought nothing of it until a few weeks ago when she mysteriously reappeared at Chidden Park. We took a walk along the canal, and that's when she asked me to spy on Callum and Lady Geraldine. She said that she'd pay me for my trouble."

"How did she explain what it was for?" asked Pixley.

"She said it was all very hush-hush, and that she couldn't tell me what it was all about. I politely declined, even though the money would have been most welcome."

"But she didn't let you decline the offer, did she?" I asked.

"No. No, she didn't. She said her contacts in Cyprus could make life very hard for my family. She also said she'd make sure I was deported if I didn't do as she said."

Pixley let out a low whistle. "What a little devil."

"Quite." Atina wrinkled her nose at the prone figure of Whittle on the floor. "At first, it was simple tasks, like listening in on conversations and telephone calls and reporting them to Ainsley."

My ears perked up. "To Ainsley? Why not to Whittle?"

"To protect herself, of course. And though I never had confirmation of this, I had the sense she'd also duped Ainsley into believing this was some cloak-and-dagger spy operation."

"Ainsley would love that, wouldn't he?" I said.

"So this divide we sensed between Whittle and Ainsley isn't true," said Pixley. "What we saw that day in Pari's cottage when Fina accused him of spying on us wasn't untrue, but it wasn't the whole story. Whittle was still calling the shots."

"Yes, she's a master manipulator," Atina said.

"Go on," said Ruby. "Tell us what happened at the gala."

"After spying on Callum and Lady Geraldine, Whittle gave me the final assignment: to kill Beryl Triggs."

I frowned at Whittle's figure on the floor. "So Whittle concocted this scheme with the brooch? But she wasn't actually killed with a cyanide-covered brooch?"

"No, it was with my syringe."

"But how?" I protested. "You were miles away from Beryl when she would have been poisoned."

"Not to mention Ruby's point about Beryl screaming if you came at her with a syringe."

"Eugenol. Cloves," said Ruby. "That's what I smelled near Beryl earlier, and I couldn't figure out why."

"Is that why you were looking for a clove cigarette at the enclosure?" I asked.

"Precisely, Feens. I'd smelled cloves in the air and assumed it was mulled wine. But no one was drinking mulled wine, and the cider didn't smell like cloves."

"True," I said, remembering the same sensation I'd had, but had made nothing of at the time.

Ruby turned to Atina. "You used the clove oil as a local anaesthetic to dull the pain of the syringe, didn't you?"

"Whittle instructed me to prick Beryl—"

"With the syringe?" asked Pixley.

"No. First, I was to prick her with an ordinary needle – without any poison on it. Something that would feel like an insect bite. So when I was passing her and no one was looking ..."

"An easy feat, as no one wanted to look at Beryl since she'd give them another task," I put in.

"Yes. I pricked Beryl near her neck when she was bending over, and she gave a little yelp. Since I was on the spot, all I had to say was that I'd noticed a wasp buzzing about. One of those lazy, drunken wasps you still see in October. Then I told her I'd give her some medicine for it, so we went into another room and shut the door. I put on the clove ointment I had as a local anaesthetic, and then jabbed her with the syringe in the back of the neck."

"I understand how she would agree to the clove oil," said

Pixley, "but how did you convince her that jabbing her was appropriate?"

Atina shrugged. "She didn't object when I told her it was to help make sure the sting didn't become infected."

"Clever," said Ruby. "No one questions a nurse, do they?"

"If this is true, then why didn't Beryl die well before we were at the enclosure?" I asked.

Ruby coughed. "It was something that had been bothering me about the poison. Cyanide is fast-acting, but generally not as quickly as the brooch story had us believe. It was possible, but unlikely."

"But then anyone might have murdered Beryl beforehand," said Pixley.

This time, Atina intervened, bizarrely arguing for her own guilt. She was proud of her cleverness. "No, no. Because as Ruby pointed out, the reasons you can jab someone with a needle are few and far between. The same logic applies as it did before."

"And Lady Geraldine must have been considerably easier to kill," said Ruby quietly. "Whittle must have been worried that Lady Geraldine knew you had killed Beryl. And her memory came in fits and starts, so she could have known even more than she was telling."

A mixture of vitriol and pain scored Atina's unlined face. "I hated Lady Geraldine, but I wasn't cruel. I gave her a sleeping draught so she didn't feel anything."

"Weren't you worried the coroner would detect the sleeping draught as a cause of death?" I asked.

"No. Besides, it was just enough to kill her but it was still a borderline amount. I knew how much she could tolerate, so I gave her a very precise amount that would go undetected. And then I put her in the canal."

"What about the bump on the back of her head?" I asked.

"It was probably from moving her to the canal," Atina said.

A groan came from the floor, but Whittle soon slumped back into her stupor.

"But I don't understand," said Pixley. "How did you make Whittle admit to setting this up, Ruby?"

"Ruby had proof of Alfreda Whittle's relationship to Fina Whittle, Callum's wife."

Ruby handed me the piece of paper she'd been waving at Whittle earlier.

I unfolded it, curious about the details.

The crumpled paper was blank.

Ruby had gambled that Whittle wouldn't look, and she had won.

CHAPTER
Thirty-Two

A BRITTLE LEAF drifted gently into my lap. Another fell onto Ruby's jaunty green hat. A third lodged itself in Pixley's teacup.

"Oi!" Pixley fished the leaf out of his teacup, shaking it onto the floor. "That's the worst of the countryside. Things are always popping up, popping off, and popping into … your tea."

"True." Ruby sipped her tea. "But it is glorious, you must admit."

We were sitting on the deck of Pixley's narrowboat in the waning warmth of an early November afternoon. Pixley had wanted to treat us to a slap-up tea at the Randolph Hotel, but had suddenly discovered a severe drought in his bank account. So we had happily settled for a delicious assortment of sandwiches, teacakes, and scones from our local baker.

"It's a crying shame I cannot publish this story – it would really bolster the old bank balance." He sighed.

Ruby pointed her teaspoon at him. "Nothing doing, young Hayford. You know as well as I that it would only cause more harm, and there's certainly been enough of that."

Pixley whinged, "But maybe just a teensy titbit for a gossip column?"

"Even if you were to publish something, would anyone

believe you, Pix?" I asked. "'Police officer coerces nurse into killing village woman with syringe and then bumps off her charge'?"

"I'd make it a snappier headline than that, Red." Pixley sniffed. "Do give me some credit."

I set down my teacup. "Are you done complaining, Pix? Because I'd like to hear how Ruby kept us out of the clink."

"Or worse." Pixley bit into a pink teacake.

"Well, first things first. Atina is returning to Cyprus."

"What?" exclaimed Pixley. "She's not going to trial?"

"Drink your tea," I said to Pixley. "Clearly you need more caffeine to rev up the old grey cells."

Pixley wrinkled his nose at me. "All right, clever clogs, tell us why Atina Kattos will get away with murder."

"I don't think she's getting away with anything," I said. "After all, she has committed two murders and will have to live with that knowledge for the rest of her life."

"So? Tell that to all the chaps locked up in Dartmoor. I'm sure they'd be just fine walking around free – even with that on their conscience."

"I'm on Feens's side," said Ruby. "I believe she does have a conscience, and one might argue that she was simply the weapon Whittle used to kill."

"Like an assassin?" asked Pixley, still unconvinced. "Even then, assassins still face trial."

"But an assassin is generally someone who is hired, or in pursuit of a cause," I said. "They're taking the initiative – they're getting money or satisfaction from killing. In Atina's case, she had good reason to believe that one of her family members might be killed if she didn't agree to Whittle's plan."

"Feens is right."

Bolstered by the warm glow of Ruby's approval, I continued. "And Whittle would never let Atina go to trial, because then she'd be exposed."

"Precisely," said Ruby.

Pixley brushed crumbs from his lap. "So everyone gets off scot-free. I see."

A silence fell over our gathering. A strained yet still companionable silence.

Pixley slapped his knee. "But there must be a way of getting at Whittle. She can't get away with this."

Ruby rubbed her brow. "Believe me, I've gone round and round in circles on this. I even thought of speaking to Ainsley about it, but I couldn't figure out how it would help."

"How about the post-mortem report?" I asked. "It wasn't complete when you made the initial accusations about the brooch, but surely it's been published since then. Wouldn't it debunk the theory of the cyanide in the glass since they can tell whether she drank the cyanide or was injected?"

"I suspect Whittle simply suppressed that part of the report." Ruby rubbed her chin. "Even if she didn't, and the report does show that Beryl was injected with cyanide, it still doesn't prove who did it."

"What if we simply told the head whatsit of the police that Atina and Whittle were in it together?" I asked. "Even risking exposing ourselves?"

"They'd never believe us, and all we'd do is get ourselves locked up," said Pixley. "For our activities, I mean."

The gravel crunched on the pathway. I shaded my eyes from the sun and squinted at the figure lumbering towards us.

It was the postman, Tom. Ruby's admirer, looking sheepish as always.

"Miss Dove, I hope it's all right that I brought your post down to you here."

"That's most kind of you, Tom. And please, do call me Ruby."

Tom flushed with pleasure and handed over a stack of letters.

Smoothing his moustache, he said, "I had a good feeling about your post this morning, Miss – erm, Ruby."

"Really?" asked Pixley. "Do you have the second sight?"

The slight tinge of irony was completely lost on Tom.

"My mum says I do, and my great-aunt Gladys had it, too."

Ruby rocketed from her seat, grabbing Tom and kissing him on the forehead. "You beauty, you little beauty!"

I couldn't tell if she was referring to Tom or the letter in her hand. I assumed it must be the latter. Or rather, the letter.

"Well, I, erm," Tom mumbled.

"Well done, young Tom," said Pixley, as if he were an ancient elder.

"Did you win the Irish sweeps?" Tom scratched his head. "Or maybe you won a contest?"

Ruby handed me the letter. "Oh yes, we won a contest of sorts, Tom. Thank you for bringing us the good news." She glanced at me, giving me a tiny nod.

Patting Tom on the shoulder, Ruby said, "Why I don't I fix you a cup of tea at the cottage and you can tell me all about your second sight and your great-aunt Gertrude."

"Aunt Gladys, Miss. Erm, Ruby."

"Right. And I believe I have a new packet of chocolate digestives as well."

Resisting the siren call of the chocolate digestives, I stayed put, scanning the letter.

As soon as Ruby and Tom were out of sight, Pixley said, "Well, have at it, Red. What does the magical missive say?"

I cleared my throat, avoiding the catch in my voice:

Dear Fina, Ruby, and Pixley,

I sent this letter to Ruby's cottage, with the hope it will find at least one of you.

When I last saw Fina, I told her that "he was spying" on the three of you, and to not let "him" get away with it. I was partially correct. At the time, I believed it was Sergeant Ainsley, who was indeed spying on you. I thought Whittle was oblivious to this, mostly because she was a woman in the police force and was unlikely to be notified by her male colleagues of their various schemes.

And whilst Ainsley was spying on you, I was mistaken about Whittle. Very mistaken.

Given what I know about her now, I have little doubt she is somehow mixed up in these two murders. I'm certain Ruby has already cracked the case given her brilliant deductive skills.

But what I do know is this: Chief Inspector Whittle has her fingers in more than one pie. In fact, I'm aware of something about her that has already allowed me to convince her to erase particular details from the murder case in Cornwall that implicate me. I have few qualms about this because I'm innocent of any involvement in that crime. Now that I have achieved that aim, it is time to expose Chief Inspector Whittle to some of her own medicine.

As I strongly suspect her of being at the heart of these murders but have no firm evidence of it, the best course of action is to give you my knowledge of her with the hope that Pixley can publish it, thereby forcing the police to launch a full-scale investigation.

After asking friends about police scandal rumours, I heard Whittle's name mentioned in connection with a tragic case of drowning ten years ago. In that case, a young woman the same age as Whittle drowned whilst on a police training course. My friend knew a fellow officer at the time who not only suspected foul play, but had witnessed Whittle actually drowning the young woman. This officer was too afraid to come forward at the time but just died a few months ago. On his deathbed, he gave my friend written testimony about what he had witnessed, including a few key facts that demonstrated his reliability.

Now, my friend didn't know what to do with this testimony – he believed the police would simply ignore it, and doubted that a newspaper would trust it. But given Pixley's position, this evidence might be just sensational enough to force the police to conduct an internal investigation, one that focuses on Whittle.

As they say, it's a long shot, but it's well worth it if it is impossible to connect her to these recent murders. The written testimony is enclosed.

If you're wondering what will happen to me, have no fear. I have good friends, and will contact you again once it's safe to do so.

Ever yours,
Niall

Pixley outstretched his hand. "Let me have a look at that testimony."

I wiped away a tear and handed it to Pixley.

"Cheer up, Red," he said, scanning the pages. "It all seems genuine enough, and I'm certain the delicious Niall will be in touch with you soon."

Ruby returned with a pot of tea and a mound of chocolate digestives.

"Don't tease her, Pix," she said. "This is the best news we've had in a long time."

"What will happen to him?" I asked.

"Who, Ainsley?" asked Pixley.

"No—"

"He's teasing you again, Feens," said Ruby. "I expect Niall will be in touch, especially if we tell him about our plans."

"Plans? What plans?" I asked. "Aren't you retired and taking up fishing?"

Ruby grinned the widest smile I'd seen in months. "When I made tea for Tom at the cottage, I received a telephone call. The stars must be in alignment."

Pixley squinted his eyes shut. "Let me guess. The King is coming to tea."

Ignoring him, she went on. "A space opened in the village that would be perfect for my design shop."

"Shouldn't that be in London?" asked Pixley. "Crickle Hythe is lovely, but it's not exactly the metropolis."

"That's what makes it so unique, although it's quite reachable from London," said Ruby. "I'm keen to give village life a go."

"Even after this affair at Chidden Park?"

"I like Pari, Miranda, and the rest of them. I could see myself settling down here."

"Settling down?" I asked.

"You?" Pixley put in.

"Absolutely. I'll focus all my energies on the latest fashions." Then she laughed. "As I said before, nothing much ever happens in an English village."

The End

Thank you for reading *Murder in a Mask!*

Positive reviews help readers discover this book. If you enjoyed *Murder in a Mask*, I'd be grateful for a review (Australia, Canada, Germany, United Kingdom, or United States).

You can also leave a positive review on Goodreads.

If you want updates and goodies, please join my reader group!

More Mysteries

The Ruby Dove Mystery Series follows the early adventures of our intrepid amateur-spy sleuths:

Book 1: The Mystery of Ruby's Sugar
Book 2: The Mystery of Ruby's Smoke
Book 3: The Mystery of Ruby's Stiletto
Book 4: The Mystery of Ruby's Tracks
Book 5: The Mystery of Ruby's Mistletoe
Book 6: The Mystery of Ruby's Roulette
Book 7: The Mystery of Ruby's Mask
Ruby Dove Mysteries Box Set 1
Ruby Dove Mysteries Box Set 2

WITH MANY CASES under their fashionable belts, Ruby and Fina are ready for more in *Partners in Spying Mysteries:*

Fatal Festivities: A Christmas Novella
Book 1: Death in Velvet
Book 2: The Art of Murder
Book 3: Murder in a Mask

About the Author

Rose Donovan is a lifelong devotee of golden age mysteries. She now travels the world seeking cosy spots to write, new adventures to inspire devious plot twists, and adorable animals to petsit.

www.rosedonovan.com
rose@rosedonovan.com
Reader Group
Follow me on Bookbub
Follow me on Goodreads

Note about UK Style

Readers fluent in US English may believe words such as "fuelled", "signalled", "hiccough", "fulfil", "titbit", "oesophagus", "blinkers", and "practise" are typographical errors in this text. Rest assured this is simply British spelling. There are also spacing and punctuation formatting differences, including periods after quotation marks in certain circumstances.

If you find any errors, I always appreciate an email so I can correct them! Please email me at rose@rosedonovan.com.

Printed in Great Britain
by Amazon